AMOS DARAGON

BOOK ONE
THE MASK WEARER

www.amosdaragon.co.uk

Originally published in Canada by Les Intouchables MMIII

First published in Great Britain by Scribo MMIX,
Scribo, a division of Book House, an imprint of
The Salariya Book Company
25 Marlborough Place, Brighton, BN1 1UB
www.salariya.com

Book Design by David Salariya

Printed and bound in Malta

Cover Illustration by David Frankland

Editor: Kathy Elgin

The text for this book is set in Cochin
The display types are set in CCNearMyth-Legends

AMOS
DARAGON

BOOK ONE

THE MASK
WEARER

BRYAN PERRO

English Edition by
Kathy Elgin

Scribo
A division of Book House

BRYAN PERRO

Bryan Perro was born in Shawinigan, Quebec, in 1968. He has trained as a drama teacher and actor, as well as obtaining a masters degree in Education. His best-selling series, *Amos Daragon*, has been translated into 19 languages (including English) and book one, *The Mask Wearer*, has sold over one million copies in Quebec alone. Perro has been awarded a variety of prizes for his fiction, including the 2006 Quebec Youth Prize for Fiction and Fantasy.

Amos Daragon
The Mask Wearer
PROLOGUE

Tales about masks of power can be found in most of the ancient legends. These masks were highly prized. They bore the sacred magic of the elements and were only given to humans of great courage and spirit. There were four masks: the mask of earth, the mask of air, the mask of fire, and the mask of water. There were also sixteen stones of power, that gave the masks their potent magic. In the eternal struggle between good and evil, day and night, and the gods of the good and evil worlds, it was the task of a chosen few to re-establish the balance between these forces. Amos Daragon, son of Urban and Frilla Daragon, was one of the chosen. On the day of his birth the supreme goddess of the world, the Lady in White, wrote his fate in golden letters in the great history of eternal heroes. Then she waited patiently for the day he would begin to fulfil his destiny.

CHAPTER ONE

THE BAY OF CAVES

The Kingdom of Omain was magnificent. It consisted of a small city lined with tidy streets over which a dark stone castle towered. High mountains, eternally capped with snow, surrounded the city. A long, wide river cascaded down through the snow-capped mountains and flowed right into the centre of the city which nestled in the valley.

There was a small fishing port in Omain, filled with brightly coloured little boats. When night fell, the people were lulled to sleep by the sound of the ocean waves. Every morning, dozens of fishermen made their way down to the river. Raising the triangular sails on their vessels, they ventured out to sea to try their luck with their lines and nets.

Along the dirt streets of Omain people travelled on foot and by donkey. The city's inhabitants were poor, with the exception of Lord Edonf. He lived in the castle and ruled over this corner of paradise with an iron fist, forcing every family to pay him huge taxes. Every month when the moon was full, the lord's personal guard entered the city to collect the money. Anyone unable to pay on demand was immediately strung up in an iron cage in the marketplace for all to see. A prisoner could remain there for days or weeks on end without food or water, and with no shelter from the cold, the heat, or vicious insects. The people knew that being condemned to the cage was tantamount to a death sentence, so they were always scrupulous when it came to paying their taxes to the lord.

Lord Edonf was as fat as a whale. He had bulging eyes, a cavernous mouth and pimply, greasy skin, all of which made him look like one of the enormous sea toads that invaded the port of Omain every year in the spring. Besides being frighteningly ugly, it was rumoured that he had a brain the size of a tadpole. Sitting by the fire, the elders told the children stories about his ridiculous antics. These tales, spun over time and embroidered by skilful storytellers, delighted both young and old.

Everyone in Omain knew, for example, the story of Yak the Troubadour. Arriving in the town with his troupe of travelling acrobats, Yak had passed himself off as a famous doctor. He persuaded Lord Edonf that swallowing sugar-coated sheep droppings would cure his failing memory. This went on for nearly a month before Lord Edonf recovered his senses. But he never forgot the so-called doctor – or the taste of sheep manure. And after that, Omain's storytellers always told the children that if they didn't obey their parents, they would get a taste of Yak's medicine. This ensured that the children of Omain had remarkably good memories.

It was in this kingdom that Amos Daragon was born. His father and mother were skilled craftspeople who had spent many long years travelling from country to country in their quest to find the ideal place to settle. When they came across the splendid kingdom of Omain, they thought it was the perfect place to live out the rest of their lives.

They were good people. However, they made the unfortunate mistake of building their little thatched cottage on the edge of a forest not far from the city. What they didn't know was that they had built their home on Lord Edonf's private land, and without his permission. When Edonf heard what they had done he sent his men to arrest them, take them to the cage, and burn down their home. Urban Daragon pleaded with Edonf's men, offering to work for the lord in exchange for their lives, and to pay off the cost of the trees they had cut down to build their little cottage. Lord Edonf accepted the offer, but now twelve years had passed since that terrible day, and Amos' father was still paying for his mistake with the sweat of his brow.

After spending so many years serving Lord Edonf, Urban was a pitiful sight. He was visibly wasting away. Lord Edonf treated him like a slave and was always ordering him to work harder. Over the past few years he had taken to beating Urban with his staff to make him work even faster. The lord of Omain took great pleasure in these beatings, and Urban, as the prisoner of his debt, had no choice but to put up with his tyranny. Every day Amos' father came home with his head hanging low and his limbs black and blue. Since he had neither money to flee the kingdom, nor the strength to stand up to Lord Edonf and cast off his shackles, Urban left home every morning in tears and came back every evening broken and bloodied.

The Daragon family was the poorest in the village, and their cottage the smallest. The walls were just made of tree trunks with the rough edges taken off and stacked together. To keep in the heat from the fireplace, Urban had stopped up any gaps with moss and hay. The straw roof was watertight, and the big stone chimney, huge in proportion to the cottage, seemed to be the only part of the building that was truly solid. A flower garden that hardly got any sun because of the large trees surrounding it and a small outbuilding that vaguely resembled a barn made up the rest of the family homestead. The cottage was sparsely furnished with a wooden table, three chairs, and bunk beds. The chimney covered almost the entire east wall, and a kettle always hung on its hook over the fire. For the Daragon family, life in their tiny cottage was a constant struggle against the elements, and against hunger and poverty.

Since he was very young, Amos had had no choice but to get by as best he could. As a result, he had developed many talents. He hunted pheasant and hares in the forest, fished in the river with his homemade rod, and collected shellfish along the seashore. It was largely thanks to him that the family managed to survive, even though on some days there wasn't much food on the table.

Over time, Amos had developed a foolproof way of catching wild birds. He would tie a slipknot in the end of a rope and hang it over the tip of a long Y-shaped pole. When he spotted a partridge or some other game bird, all he had to do was keep his distance and then, at the right moment, quickly and silently slip the snare over the bird's neck and yank the rope. Thanks to this technique, many a partridge found its way onto the family dinner table.

Amos had learned to listen to nature, to blend in with the bracken and walk in the forest without making a sound. He was at home with the trees and knew all the best places to find wild berries. By the time he was twelve he could track all the forest animals. Sometimes, during the cold season, he was even able to unearth truffles, those delicious underground mushrooms that grew at the foot of oak trees. The forest held no secrets for him.

But Amos was deeply unhappy. Every day he stood by as his father suffered and his mother sank deeper and deeper into despair. His parents, constantly penniless, argued a lot. Immersed in the misery of their daily lives, they no longer held any hope of escape. When they were young, Urban and Frilla had always dreamed of travelling. They had wanted more than anything to live their lives happy and free. But their eyes, which had once sparkled so brightly, were now dull with sadness and fatigue. Amos dreamed every night of rescuing his parents from their torment and giving them a better life. Also, since Urban and Frilla were too poor to send him to school, the boy dreamed of finding a teacher who would help him to understand the world, answer his questions and advise him what books to read. Every night Amos Daragon sighed as he fell asleep, hoping that the next day would bring him a new life.

One fine summer morning Amos went to the seashore to gather mussels and catch crabs. He followed his usual route but without much success. His meagre findings, carried in one of his two wooden buckets, were certainly not enough to feed three people. 'Well,' he said to himself, 'it looks like there's nothing much left along this section of shore. But it's still early and the sun is shining, so let's see what I can find further on.'

He first considered heading north towards an area he did not know very well, but then he remembered the Bay of Caves. This was quite a distance from where he was, and away to the south. Having been there a few times already, Amos knew he would not be able to spend much time scavenging, but if he walked quickly, he could get home before evening, as he had promised his father.

The Bay of Caves was an extraordinary place. Over time, the waves had eroded the rock and the tides had carved out grottoes, basins and magnificent sculptures. Amos had discovered it quite by accident, and each time he went there he went home with large quantities of crabs and mussels. He didn't go there very often, though, because it was such a long way to walk, and returning home with a bucket in each hand filled to overflowing was never easy.

After walking for two hours, Amos finally reached the Bay of Caves. Weary from his journey, he sat down on the pebble beach and looked at the amazing landscape. The tide was low and the enormous sculptures carved by the ocean stood over the bay like petrified giants. Everywhere along the cliff, Amos could see deep holes dug by thousands of years of tides, waves and storms. The sun, already high in the sky, beat down on him, but the breeze from the sea cooled his tanned skin.

'Come on,' he said to himself. 'Time to get to work!'

Amos quickly filled his two buckets with crabs. There were dozens more on the beach, taken by surprise by the ebbing tide and now struggling to return to the safety of the sea. As the young fisherman was walking past a cave entrance which was wider and higher than the others, he noticed a big, black raven lying dead on the beach. Amos looked up at the sky and saw twenty or so more ravens flying in circles above the cliff.

'Those birds are circling,' he thought, 'waiting for something to die so they can feed on the carcass. It could be a big fish, or maybe there's a beached whale nearby. This poor raven was unlucky. It must have flown into the rocks and broken its neck.'

Looking around for a dying animal, Amos noticed three more ravens a little closer to the entrance of the cave. These were very much alive. They were staring into the cave as if they were trying to make out something deep inside the stone walls. As Amos went closer to see what they were doing, he heard a loud cry from deep inside the cave. At once, the three birds fell dead, the life knocked out of them by the terrible sound.

Amos himself was blown over by the force of the blast. He collapsed as though he had received a violent blow. Instinctively, he covered his ears with his hands and lay curled on the ground, his heart pounding. His legs refused to budge. Never before had he heard such a sound. It seemed to him both human and animal, and it must have come from an extremely powerful source. Then an enchanting voice, soft and melodious, snapped Amos out of his daze. It was as though a lyre had suddenly started playing from deep inside the cave.

'Don't be afraid, young man. I am not an enemy.'

Amos lifted his head and struggled to his feet.

'I'm in the cave. Come quickly. I'm waiting for you. I won't hurt you. I only shouted to chase away the birds.'

Slowly, Amos walked into the cave. The voice continued to sound and its words chimed in his ears like a symphony of little bells.

'Don't be afraid. I don't trust those birds because they're nosy and crude. They're always spying, and they love eating fish far too much for my liking. When you see me, you will understand why I say this. Rest assured that I mean you no harm. Come quickly now, for I haven't much time left.'

In the darkness, Amos moved deeper and deeper into the cave, groping his way towards the voice. Suddenly, the ground and the rough stone walls were bathed in a soft blue light, making the small puddles of water gleam and the wet walls shimmer in different shades of blue. It was magnificent. The light filled the inside of the cave, giving Amos the feeling that he was walking through glowing liquid. The voice continued:

'Isn't it beautiful? It is the light of my people. By sheer force of will, my people can produce light from salt water. Turn around. I'm right over here.'

When Amos looked closely at the creature, it took all his courage to keep from running away. Before his eyes, a real mermaid lay in a puddle of water. Her long hair was the pale colour of a sunset as it dipped behind the ocean. Strong and beautiful, she wore on her breast a shield of shells that resembled a soldier's armour. Between the armour and her skin, Amos thought he saw a shirt woven from seaweed. Her nails were long and pointed, and her body ended in a magnificent fish-tail, thick and heavy. Close to her lay a weapon, an ivory trident, carved from a narwhal horn and decorated with light red coral. The mermaid smiled as she spoke:

'I see the fear in your eyes, but please don't be alarmed. I know that creatures like myself have a bad reputation among humans. Your legends tell of mermaids bewitching sailors and luring them to the bottom of the sea. You must believe me when I tell you this is not true! It is the merrows who do this. Although our bodies are similar, merrows are repulsively ugly.

Like mermaids, the merrows use their voices to enchant men. But then they devour their victims, loot cargoes and raise storms that sink ships, which they then make into their homes at the bottom of the ocean.'

As the mermaid spoke, Amos noticed large gashes in her armour.

'Are you hurt?' he asked. 'I'm sure I can help you. Let me go into the forest. I know where to find plants that will heal you.'

The mermaid smiled warmly.

'You are kind, young man, but I know I will die very soon. I was badly injured in a battle with the merrows, and my wounds are deep. Where I come from, deep under the ocean waves, the war against evil creatures has been raging for many, many days. Now, take this white stone and, as soon as you can, go and find Queen Gwenfadrilla in Tarkasis Forest. Tell the queen that her friend Crivannia, Princess of the Waters, is dead, and her kingdom has fallen into enemy hands. Also, tell her that I have chosen you to be a mask wearer. She will understand and act accordingly. Swear to me, on your life, that you will carry out this mission.'

Without even thinking, Amos swore on his life.

'Go quickly now. Run and cover your ears. When a Princess of the Waters dies, she leaves this world with a terrible sound. Go! Run! May the power of the elements be with you every step of the way! Take this ivory trident – it will be useful to you.'

Amos ran from the cave. Just in time, he covered his ears with both hands. A gruesome, sorrowful song, heavy with suffering and melancholy, echoed through the bay, making the ground tremble. Rocks began to fall all around him, then, with a terrifying crash, the cave in which the mermaid lay collapsed. When it was all over, a deafening silence reigned.

As he climbed back up the cliff with the ivory trident tucked under his arm and a bucket full of crabs in each hand, Amos turned to gaze at the place one last time. Somehow he knew that he would never see the Bay of Caves again. Then, as he watched, he realised he was looking at hundreds of mermaids, their heads bobbing out of the water, watching over the princess's tomb from a distance. It was only after he had walked several miles towards home, that Amos heard a dirge carried by the wind. A choir of mermaids, paying their final homage to Princess Crivannia.

CHAPTER TWO

LORD EDONF, THE STONE SOUP, AND THE HORSES

When Amos arrived home late in the afternoon, he was very surprised to find Lord Edonf and two guards there. In front of the cottage stood his parents, their heads bowed in submission, silently enduring Lord Edonf's insults. The fat, ugly man was crimson with rage and was threatening to burn down their home. He accused the couple of farming without his permission and hunting on his land. In addition, he said, the family had in their possession a donkey that belonged to him. The animal had apparently been stolen from inside his castle.

On this point, Lord Edonf was not mistaken. During a brief night-time visit to the castle, Amos had rescued the donkey to save it from cruel treatment. He had told his parents that he'd found it lost in the woods, and it had followed him home. Of course, he had not confessed his crime. Lord Edonf was now demanding a huge sum of money from Amos' parents as restitution. Urban and Frilla were obviously unable to pay and didn't know what to say or do.

Fearing for their lives, Amos slipped quietly into the cottage. He couldn't stand to see his mother and father humiliated in this way. Things would have to change for him and his family, and he knew it was up to him to do something. If he didn't act now, he never would. But what could he do? How could they escape from this place which had become a living hell? He looked around desperately, hoping to come up with an idea or a trick that would get Lord Edonf off their backs once and for all.

He saw that his mother had put the big iron kettle on the fire to boil water. Frilla Daragon had planned to make soup with whatever her son might bring home. Suddenly, Amos had a brilliant idea. It was a very risky one but, summoning up all his courage, he decided to act. Wrapping his hands in a thick cloth so that he wouldn't burn himself, Amos grabbed the kettle handle. Without being seen, he carried the large kettle out to the garden, not far from where Lord Edonf and his men stood. He set it down on the ground, picked up a dead twig and began a strange ritual. He danced around the kettle, hitting the side of it with his stick and repeating with each blow:

'Boil, soup, boil!'

In his anger, Lord Edonf did not immediately notice Amos. It was only with the seventh or eighth repetition of 'Boil, soup, boil!' that he stopped bellowing and took notice of what the boy was doing.

'What are you up to, you little fool?' he asked him.

'I'm boiling the water for dinner, my lord. We're going to make stone soup!' answered Amos, looking quite proud of his feat.

Puzzled, Lord Edonf looked at the boy's parents, who just smiled. They knew how clever their son was and realized that he must be cooking up something far more interesting than soup.

Lord Edonf continued: 'And by what miracle can you make soup out of stones?'

Amos realised he had the big fish right on his hook and he wasn't going to let him get away. His trick seemed to be working perfectly!

'It's very simple, my good Lord Edonf. With this magic wand, I make the water in the kettle boil until it dissolves the rock. Then I wait for the broth to cool down. It makes excellent "cream of stone soup". My parents and I have eaten nothing but this for years.'

Lord Edonf guffawed loudly. He rolled up his shirtsleeve and plunged his hand into the water to test the temperature. As the scalding liquid burned his skin, his face paled and he pulled his hand out, howling in pain. Nursing the hand that was now as red as a boiled lobster, Lord Edonf pounded the ground with his feet and cursed the gods.

'Quick! Quick! Cold water! Quick! Quick! Ice water!' he yelled.

One of the guards, who had been snooping in the little barn, ran to help his master. Without hesitating, he grabbed Edonf's arm and plunged his hand back into the kettle, thinking it might relieve the pain. With tears in his eyes, Edonf screamed: 'Let go of my hand, you fool! Let go of my hand or I'll have you hanged!'

The guard did not have a clue why he was being scolded like this, and got a sound thrashing from his master. A hard kick to his behind sent him sprawling on the ground. It was all Amos' parents could do to keep from laughing. Meanwhile, Amos made a compress for Lord Edonf's hand out of leaves and herbs. Exhausted by the whole episode, the fat lord finally calmed down and said, in a feeble voice: 'I want that wand that makes the water boil. Give me that wand and I will allow you to farm and hunt on all the land you want. I'll even allow you to keep the donkey!'

Amos looked very serious, although his heart was pounding in his chest. He was terribly afraid that Lord Edonf would realize he was being taken for a fool but he did not let it show. This discussion had to be handled very tactfully.

'I'm sorry, my lord, but this magic wand has belonged to my family for generations. It is our most precious possession, and my parents can't possibly live without it. Please, pretend you never saw it. Please – just burn down the house as you promised and we will go and live somewhere else, far from your kingdom.'

Grimacing with pain, Lord Edonf stood up and took ten gold pieces from his purse.

'This is what I offer you for your magic wand. If you refuse this money, I will seize the wand anyway and order your cottage burned to the ground. The choice is yours! Make your mind up, boy – I'm fast approaching the end of my patience!'

His head bowed, Amos handed Lord Edonf the stick.

'May your will be done, but please know that I accept this money with a heavy heart. You must not forget, my lord, to dance around the kettle as you repeat the words 'Boil, soup, boil!' And keep it up until the water reaches boiling point.'

Lord Edonf threw the gold pieces on the ground and, grabbing the stick, got back on his horse.

'I'll remember,' he snarled. 'I'm not an idiot.'

The guards mounted their steeds and the three men galloped off. This clever trick had earned Amos the money he needed to travel to Tarkasis Forest, just as he had promised Crivannia, Princess of the Waters. But knowing full well that Lord Edonf would soon discover the deception and return, he had to come up with another bright idea. He wrapped eight of the gold pieces in hay, added a laxative herb and got the donkey to swallow the lot. Then he told his parents about his adventure at the Bay of Caves and to prove he was telling the truth, Amos showed them the white stone and the trident the mermaid had given him. Urban and Frilla immediately realised the importance of the mission that had been entrusted to their son. Full of pride, they encouraged him to journey to Tarkasis Forest to give Queen Gwenfadrilla the message from the Princess of the Waters.

Twelve long and difficult years had gone by since the Daragons had settled in Edonf's kingdom, and their instincts told them that this land had only misery and suffering to offer them. It was high time they left. As the family possessed virtually nothing, it did not take them long to pack. Then Amos said to his parents: 'Go to the clearing at the foot of the mountain. I'll join you later, and I'll bring horses.'

Clutching their meagre possessions, Urban and Frilla set off immediately to find the meeting place they had agreed on. They didn't ask any questions and had no fears about the son they were temporarily leaving behind. They knew that Amos was gifted with extraordinary intelligence and would know exactly how to shield himself from Lord Edonf's wrath. That lad had more than one trick up his sleeve!

Amos waited patiently for Lord Edonf to return. He used the time to say his goodbyes to the forest where he was born, to the little thatched cottage and to the donkey he would have to leave behind. Soon, just as he had predicted, Edonf reappeared with his two guards, and began yelling at the top of his voice: 'I'll have your head, you little rascal! I'll have you drawn and quartered, you miserable little scoundrel! I'll eat your heart for breakfast, you worthless little toad!'

Calmly, and without Edonf seeing him, Amos went into the barn. He grabbed the donkey's ears, looked the beast straight in the eyes and said: 'Donkey, give me gold! Give me gold!'

Lord Edonf and his guards went into the cottage, had a quick look round and then dashed towards the barn. As they got there, the boy's voice stopped him in their tracks.

'Let's keep quiet,' said Edonf to his guards. 'We'll surprise him.'

The three men peeped inside the barn, pressing their eyes to the gaps between the boards. What they saw was Amos rubbing the donkey's ears and repeating this same phrase over and over again: 'Give me gold! Give me gold!'

Suddenly, they saw the animal lift its tail and large dollops of dung hit the straw. Before their incredulous eyes, Amos went behind the donkey and, one by one, pulled eight gold pieces from the mess. With this, Edonf burst into the barn, drawing his sword.

'You little scoundrel! You thought you could trick me with your fake magic wand for boiling water? I made a fool of myself in front of my whole court! Until now, I could think of nothing but killing you, but I have just had a better idea. I'll take the donkey! I have heard it said, although I never really believed it, that there are magic hens that lay golden eggs. But now I see that some donkeys have an interesting way of producing gold!'

Amos frowned and answered slyly: 'Take my fortune, take my donkey, and I hope you make it gallop at top speed to your castle! That will upset its stomach and you'll get nothing but donkey droppings!'

Lord Edonf roared with satisfaction.

'You think you're so smart, you little worm? You've just given me a clue that will keep me from making a serious mistake. Guards, bring out that donkey with the greatest care! We will lead it back to the castle on foot. We'll leave the horses here and come back for them later. I'll follow on foot to make sure nothing happens to this precious creature. And if it relieves itself on the way, I'll be on hand to collect all the gold pieces. As for you, you good-for-nothing peasant, you can keep these eight coins – they're still warm! With the ten I gave you for the fake magic wand, you can consider that a very good price for the donkey.'

Sniffing, Amos begged Lord Edonf: 'No, please, my kind lord, don't do that to me. Please give me back the donkey! It's our entire fortune – it's everything we have! Kill me, but please, leave the donkey to my parents.'

Lord Edonf kicked Amos to the ground and, bending over him, growled: 'You'll just have to eat stone soup. That's your speciality, isn't it, you little fool?'

Amos watched as Lord Edonf and his two guards walked slowly away, leading the precious animal. The fat man sang and laughed blissfully. He was very pleased with himself.

A few moments later, delighted at the way things had turned out, Amos climbed onto the lord's horse. He tied the reins of the other two horses to the saddle, and rode directly to the clearing at the foot of the mountain where his father and mother were already waiting for him.

And that's how a new story began to spread through the Kingdom of Omain. The old storytellers still told the tale of Yak the Troubadour, but now the children also wanted to hear about the pranks of Amos Daragon, the crafty boy who one day traded an ordinary stick of wood for ten gold pieces, and a common donkey for three fine horses!

CHAPTER THREE

GREAT BRATEL

mos' parents already knew about Tarkasis Forest. During their early wanderings, long before the birth of their son, they had heard rumours about the place. It was said that those who dared to venture into it were never seen again. Legends told of some terrible force that lived deep in the woods. Urban Daragon told his son how, one day when he was looking for work in the little town of Berrion, he had met a very old man in the market square. The old man was desperately trying to recover his lost youth. He stopped all the passers-by and begged them: 'Sir! Madam! Please! My youth has been stolen! I have to get it back! Help me, please! I beg you. I'm just eleven years old! Just yesterday, I was a beautiful child full of life. But I woke up this morning and my youth had disappeared. Help me! Please, help me...'

Some people laughed at him, others ignored him. No one took him seriously. But Urban Daragon went up to this old man with his white hair and long white beard and asked what had happened to him. The fellow told his story.

'I lived near Tarkasis Forest. My parents had a thatched cottage at the edge of the woods. My father always warned me not to go near that cursed place, but yesterday morning I lost my dog and went looking for him. After I had looked all around the house and in the nearby fields, I heard my dog barking in the forest. I knew it was him because I recognized the way he barks when he's frightened. I ran to find him without even thinking about my parents' warning. I remember seeing many lights, like little spots of sunlight shining through the trees. Then, out of nowhere, soft, beautiful music began to play and I suddenly felt like dancing. I was waltzing with the lights, and felt happy and serene. I don't know how long it lasted, but I must have danced for a very long time because I fell asleep, I was so tired.

'When I opened my eyes there was no sign of my dog. I had this long, white beard, and realized my hair had also turned completely white and grown very long. In a panic, I ran back to my house, only to find it had disappeared, as had my parents. Everything around me had changed completely! There was a road where my father's vegetable garden used to be! In tears, I followed the road and arrived here in Berrion. This town is just a few minutes from Tarkasis Forest, yet I didn't know it existed. I'd never even heard of it. It's as if it just sprouted up overnight. I don't understand what's happening to me. I'm only eleven years old – we just celebrated my birthday! I assure you that I'm not an old man, and I'm not crazy. Please, help me to recover my youth. Help me find my parents again, my house, and my dog. Please!'

Urban told Amos that he had believed the poor man but he knew there was nothing he could do for him. Touched by his sad story, he'd gone on his way.

Since the town of Berrion was in the far north of the land, the Daragons set out again at sunrise next morning. They had slept under the stars in the clearing and were now ready for their journey. It would take them a whole month, but they had three good horses and ten gold pieces. As soon as he rejoined his parents, Amos had given his father eight of the coins, which he had carefully placed in his purse. The two other gold pieces were hidden in Amos' shoes, in case the trick with the donkey failed. Lord Edonf might just possibly have suspected it was another ruse, when he saw Amos pulling the coins from the animal's excrement. But since the lord was even more stupid than the donkey, the Daragon family's journey was being entirely financed by their former master.

Together, Amos, Urban, and Frilla left the Kingdom of Omain by the mountain pass. Following the road north, they crossed meadows and valleys, passing through poverty-stricken villages, green woods, and charming little farms. The route was long and difficult for Amos. He was not accustomed to riding for days on end, and each evening he fell into an exhausted sleep.

Along the way, Urban Daragon and his wife had bought everything they needed for their long journey. Now the family's provisions included a tent, warm blankets, and an oil lamp. Amos had never seen his father looking so happy and his mother so beautiful. With each passing day, Urban and Frilla Daragon felt more alive. It was almost as if they had slept through a very long, dark night and now they were opening their eyes and coming back to life.

With gentle and loving hands, Frilla braided her son's long hair. Urban laughed a lot, and Amos felt his father's hearty laughter resonate deep in his soul. In spite of his weariness, it was the greatest happiness he had ever known.

Amos had fun with his father, bathed in the clear waters of the streams along the way, and ate the wonderful food his mother prepared. She made him a suit of leather armour, and his father bought him an earring in the form of a wolf's head. Sitting proudly on his handsome steed with the mermaid's trident slung across his back, with his long braids and his well-fitting armour, Amos looked like a young warrior from an ancient legend. In spite of all their expenses, Urban's purse still contained six gold coins. Compared with the poverty they saw all around them, it was a fortune.

As they sat by the fire in the evening, Urban would tell Amos about his early life, his travels, and his adventures. He had been an orphan, and had to learn a trade quickly in order to survive. Then he set out 'to conquer the world', as he liked to say, laughing now at his naivety. However, he had experienced more setbacks than joys as he journeyed from place to place. The tide had turned, as he put it, the day he met Frilla. The beautiful eighteen-year-old shepherdess, with her long black hair and hazel eyes, had stolen his heart, but she was already betrothed to another man and Urban had had to run away with her so that they could be together. After that, a lucky star shone on the young couple's life together and for eight years Urban and Frilla lived happily, travelling freely from one village to another and from one kingdom to the next. The birth of their child brought them even greater happiness. The twelve years of misery that followed in the Kingdom of Omain had been a terrible experience that they would try to forget as quickly as possible.

Two weeks into their travels, the Daragon family met a knight on the road. He carried a broad sword and a shield emblazoned with the image of a shining sun. His armour shone in the sunlight like a mirror.

'Halt!' cried the knight. 'Identify yourselves immediately or you will suffer the consequences!'

Very politely, Urban Daragon introduced himself and explained that the family were on their way to Berrion, in the north. He and his wife were travelling craftspeople, he added, and they had decided to take to the road again after living for many years in the Kingdom of Omain where Lord Edonf himself had rewarded their excellent work on many occasions. Of course, it was rare to see craftsmen in possession of such beautiful horses, but this explanation seemed to satisfy the knight, who nodded his head. Urban refrained from mentioning the real reason why they were travelling to Berrion.

'Is it true that Lord Edonf of Omain is as stupid as a mule?' asked the knight, laughing.

'You're insulting mules by comparing them to Lord Edonf,' answered Amos. 'At least they're good workers. A single knight like you could easily seize all the lands of Omain because the army is just like Lord Edonf – weak and lazy.'

'Your son has a good tongue in his head, and he knows the power of a sword when he sees it,' said the knight, visibly flattered by the compliment. 'My comrades and I are out searching for wizards who are hiding somewhere in this forest. We don't know who they are, but they certainly wouldn't look like you or be as polite as you. You may pass! Continue on your way, travellers, and know that you are entering the kingdom of the Knights of the Light. Our capital, Great Bratel, is just a few leagues from here. At the gates of the city, tell the sentry that Barthelemy – that's my name – has authorized you to enter. But don't delay in getting inside. When night falls, strange things happen outside the city walls. May the light carry you! Adieu, good people.'

The Daragon family politely bade farewell to the knight and continued their journey.

Before arriving in the capital, Amos and his parents passed through two small villages set very close together. A heavy, threatening silence hung over them. Everywhere they looked, in the streets, around the houses, there appeared to be nothing but stone statues. Men, women and children stood petrified, their faces frozen in fear. Amos dismounted and touched the face of a man. It was smooth and hard, cold and lifeless. Clearly he had once been the local blacksmith. His arm was raised and he held a hammer in his hand, as though about to strike something in front of him. His beard, hair, and clothes had all turned to stone. Others had been caught trying to flee, and lay stiff on the ground. Pigs, chickens, mules, and cats had all been transformed. Even the dogs were now motionless, crouched as if poised to attack.

Something, or someone, had entered these villages and cast a spell over the inhabitants. The facial expression of each of these human statues showed only one emotion: pure terror. Without exception, they had all been petrified whilst in the grip of panic.

Suddenly, a large grey tomcat, clearly very old, emerged from behind a woodpile. It walked slowly towards the travellers and sniffed at them. Amos, taking the animal in his arms, saw at once that it was blind. This cat was the only living thing in the village that had survived the curse and the reason was obvious – it could not see. All the other people and animals must have turned to stone because they had looked at the enemy!

On closer examination, it appeared that there had been not one enemy, but many. The ground around them was criss-crossed with triangular footprints. Each footprint ended in three long toes with marks of a membrane between each toe. Amos realised that the creatures must have been walking upright on two legs, and that their feet were webbed, like those of a duck.

Urban ordered his son back onto his horse. They had nothing more to learn from this place, and the sun would soon be setting. With Frilla carrying the blind cat, the little family left the cursed village and continued their journey to Great Bratel.

Great Bratel was an impressive city. Built in the middle of farmlands, it was surrounded by massive, grey stone walls impenetrable by any army. Beyond the farmland stretched a vast forest. From high up in lookout towers, the sentries could easily see any enemy battalion approaching from at least a league in every direction. A heavy portcullis protected the enormous gates.

The travellers were halted by five sentries clad in shining armour and wielding shields emblazoned with the image of the sun. Urban Daragon identified himself and mentioned Barthelemy's name, just as the knight had told him.

The guards seemed satisfied and one of them explained: 'The gates remain open during the day, but we only raise the portcullis twice a day, once at daybreak, and again at sunset. The peasants who farm the land around the castle will soon be coming back, and you can enter the city along with them. They'll be here within the hour so you won't have long to wait. Sit down and rest. There's food and drink over there, go and help yourselves. Welcome to Great Bratel, travellers! May the light carry you!'

Thanking the sentry, the Daragons made their way over to the food. Amos took an apple and a few chestnuts and sat down near the portcullis so he could observe the city. There was a great deal of activity inside, with people hurrying to and fro and knights patrolling the streets. It looked as if the inhabitants were preparing for battle. In the public square not far from the gates, the ashes of what had been a big fire were still smouldering. Amos asked one of the sentries why they had lit such a big fire during daylight.

The guard smiled: 'Oh, we burned a witch this morning. On your way here you must have seen what happened in some of the surrounding villages. Well, Yaune the Purifier, our liege lord, thinks that it was a wizard's spell. Our men are combing the forest to flush out the culprit. Anyone who practises magic in any form is burned at the stake. We've already roasted seven people this week, including two manimals.'

'What on earth's a manimal?' asked Amos. 'I've never heard of such a thing.'

'They're humans who can transform themselves into animals. When I was very young people talked a lot about manimals, but now they're more of a legend than a reality. I never believed in them anyway, and I doubt that the man and woman we just burned had such powers.

'But nobody really knows what's happening in the kingdom. Our king is devastated. Nobody can sleep properly because every night we hear horrible noises coming from the forest. Everyone cowers in fear when night falls. I just don't know what to think. But now it's time to raise the portcullis. Farewell, young man, May the light carry you!'

'May the light carry you, too,' Amos answered.

The peasants entered Great Bratel and the Daragon family followed on behind. Urban, Frilla and Amos at once set about looking for a place to spend the night. They found an inn called The Goat's Head. It was a dark, foreboding place with dingy grey walls. Inside, it was sparsely furnished with a few tables and a long bar, at which several customers stood talking together. The atmosphere became even more ominous when the Daragons entered. They sat down in silence, feeling the heavy stares of the locals who were studying the new arrivals closely, looking them over from head to foot.

The wonderful aroma of hot soup wafted in from the kitchen and Amos' mouth watered as he sat down. The conversation soon started up again as people lost interest in them. After a few minutes, Urban waved to the innkeeper who was standing behind the bar. The man did not budge. Frilla tried to get his attention by calling to him: 'Something smells good in here! We'd like something to eat and a room for the night...'

It was no use. The man went on chatting with his other customers. Then, just as the Daragons finally decided to get up and leave, the innkeeper winked at his regulars and said loudly: 'Just a minute! You can't leave without paying!'

'But we didn't eat or drink anything, sir,' replied Urban politely. 'Why would we have to pay?'

The innkeeper, a mocking smile on his lips, continued: 'We don't serve strangers here, but it's clear that you've been enjoying the smell of my soup for quite some time. You have therefore consumed the aroma of my cooking and you'll have to pay for that. Don't think you can enjoy yourselves without coughing up some cash!'

The other customers laughed heartily. The innkeeper often used this trick to get money out of innocent travellers.

'Pay me,' the innkeeper went on, 'or you'll end up behind bars!'

Urban refused to open his purse. Three men wielding wooden clubs moved swiftly to block the exit.

'You, go and fetch a knight. We have a problem here,' the innkeeper said to one of his friends.

A few minutes later, the man came back with a knight. It was Barthelemy.

'What's going on here?' asked the exasperated knight, as he entered the inn.

'These people want to leave without paying. They inhaled the aroma of my soup, and they've offered me nothing in return. This is my inn and I have a right to sell whatever I like, even a smell. Am I right, noble knight?'

Barthelemy recognized the Daragon family right away. Embarrassed, he said to them: 'You've made a bad choice, my friends. This inn must be the worst in Great Bratel. But, according to our laws, this innkeeper is right and he knows it. He has the right to sell whatever he likes, even the smell of soup. All the travellers who stop here at The Goat's Head are swindled. The innkeeper uses the law to full advantage – he's a crook, but I can't do anything about it. I have to make sure that he is paid for the smell of his cooking. In case of a dispute, it is the knights who serve as judges and who decide on these issues. Just leave him something and go. I can't help you.'

'Fine,' sighed Amos. 'We will pay the innkeeper properly.'

Laughter resounded throughout the inn. The trick always worked perfectly and all the customers were enjoying the show.

Grabbing his father's purse, Amos continued: 'In this purse, we have exactly six gold pieces. Would that be enough to pay for the smell of a soup we didn't even taste?'

The innkeeper rubbed his hands, delighted. 'Why yes, of course, young man! That would be perfect!'

Amos held the purse up to the scoundrel's ear and jingled the coins.

'Since we inhaled the smell of a soup we didn't eat,' he said, 'well then, we'll pay with the sound of coins you won't pocket!'

Barthelemy laughed aloud. 'I have witnessed the fact that this boy has just discharged his debt and that of his parents!'

The innkeeper stood open-mouthed. He was humiliated at having been tricked by a mere child but he couldn't protest. Laughing heartily, Amos and his parents, accompanied by Barthelemy, left the inn. The snickering from inside was replaced by a heavy silence.

CHAPTER FOUR

BEORF

t the suggestion of their new friend, Amos and his parents took a room at a pretty inn owned by Barthelemy's mother. Spacious, well kept, and surrounded by magnificent rose bushes, the fine red-stone building stood a fair distance from the city centre.

The Daragons were happy to rest at last. The old, blind tomcat they had adopted soon found a quiet corner and settled down to snooze in peace.

Urban managed to find work at the inn. After the death of Barthelemy's father, the knight had tried to take care of the building himself but, despite his best efforts, he was no handyman. The roof needed mending and Urban gladly agreed to fix the clumsy repairs. In exchange, the Daragons were given a large, comfortable, well-lit room. And if Frilla were willing to help out in the kitchen – which she eagerly agreed to do – they would be fed, too. Once these arrangements had been made, the Daragons quickly settled into their new lodgings.

The inn was called The Arms and the Sword. It was the knights' favourite meeting place, where they gathered to share a drink, play cards or discuss their most recent battles. From sunrise to twilight there was always someone around who was willing to recount a feat of arms or brag about an exploit. Some came to relax between missions. The kingdom was always being invaded by barbarians from the north, and there had been many skirmishes. Barthelemy's father had himself been a great knight and died in combat, but he lived on in the memories of his comrades in arms, who often recounted his exploits. His widow was always moved by these tales.

Any knight from a neighbouring kingdom who was passing through Berrion stopped at The Arms and the Sword to exchange the latest news and boast about his skill as a swordsman. It was a lively place, always teeming with people and echoing with laughter, where the most fantastic tales could be heard at any time of day. Yaune the Purifier, Lord of Great Bratel and master of the Knights of the Light, often dropped in, either to relax or to speak with his men. For a curious boy like Amos there couldn't have been a better place to stay than this inn, where all the kingdom's breaking news was first heard.

All the talk now was of the spell that had been cast over the villages. Nobody could explain what had turned all the inhabitants into stone statues but, as a precaution, the neighbouring countryside had been evacuated. Those peasants who had stayed in their homes despite the warnings – in fact, anyone who spent the night outside the city walls – had fallen under the evil spell. Cavalry detachments combing the forest regularly came across sparrows, owls, deer and wolves that had turned to stone. There was much talk about a battalion sent by a neighbouring kingdom to assist Great Bratel – it too, had been found petrified. The bloodcurdling screams coming from the depths of the woods every night did little to reassure people. These piercing cries chilled them to the bone, especially as each night these sounds edged a little closer to the city walls. The knights felt that they were facing an invisible enemy shrouded in darkness. There was no way the enemy could be one individual, but all those who had been victim to its power were now locked in silence. However much the knights would have liked to hear the truth about what had happened, the stone statues revealed nothing. Barthelemy and his companions were just as concerned as the townspeople. Yaune the Purifier seemed to be grasping at straws, burning more and more alleged witches and false wizards at the stake. No one had any idea how to defeat this shadowy evil.

A week had passed since Amos and his parents had arrived in the city. Although they were content with their life here, they felt they had already spent too much time in Great Bratel. They began making plans to set out once more for Tarkasis Forest. News of the trick Amos had used at The Goat's Head had quickly spread among the knights. Barthelemy had taken a keen pleasure in telling his companions how the young lad had outsmarted the dishonest innkeeper. Complete strangers stopped Amos in the street to congratulate him for putting the swindler in his place.

Amos often took long walks through the city. He strolled through the streets, discovering little alleys and tiny craft shops. Every morning a sprawling market was set up in a square in the middle of the city, right in front of the imposing fortified residence of Yaune the Purifier. It was there that one morning Amos noticed a boy crawling on all fours under the merchants' stalls. Just a little older than Amos, he was as round as a piglet and had straight blond hair. Amos was surprised to see that he had very bushy sideburns and, despite his large rump and rolls of fat, he was extremely agile. Quick as lightning, his hand reached out to grab fruit, pieces of meat, sausages and loaves of bread without anyone noticing. When his bag was stuffed with provisions, he fled the marketplace.

Curious, Amos decided to follow him. The fat boy turned a corner and ran towards one of the city walls, far from any houses. Once he reached the foot of the wall, he looked around cautiously – and disappeared! Amos could not believe his eyes. Carefully, he approached the spot where the boy had vanished, and found a deep hole. The boy must have jumped down into it, which explained his sudden disappearance.

Amos climbed down the hole. At the bottom he found a long, crudely dug tunnel which ran beneath the wall. Following it, Amos found himself on the other side, in tall meadow grasses. Standing on tiptoe, Amos looked around for the boy, and just caught a glimpse of his shadow as it disappeared at the edge of the distant forest. It seemed impossible that anyone could move so quickly. The boy had crossed the meadow in a flash, as fast as a man on a galloping horse. And he was carrying a huge bag of provisions!

Amos ran as fast as he could to the edge of the forest. On the ground under the trees, he saw strange tracks. There were footprints, but handprints also. Was the fat boy moving on all fours in the forest? A little further, the prints turned into the tracks of a bear cub. Suddenly it came to Amos: he had been following a manimal! That would explain the creature's impressive agility, his strength and speed. Young bears were energetic and powerful creatures – and this would also explain all the hair on the strange boy's face. So manimals weren't just legendary creatures! There really were life forms that could transform themselves at will. But there couldn't be many with such a gift.

Amos remembered the manimal couple burned in the public square. He guessed that a child who stole food probably had no parents to provide for him. The Knights of the Light must have killed his parents. They were probably seen transforming into bears, and were burned at the stake for dabbling in witchcraft. The knights must have thought that any human being that could turn itself into an animal could also turn a human into stone. 'I must find the boy and talk to him,' thought Amos.

With the mermaid's trident slung across his back, he followed the manimal's trail into the dark forest. After about an hour he reached a small clearing. The tracks led to a charming little round house built of wood. It was surrounded by beehives and thousands of bees buzzed around it.

'Is anyone there?' called Amos in a friendly voice. 'Please answer me... I'm not your enemy... I followed your tracks, young bear, and I'd like to talk to you!'

Silence. Amos saw and heard nothing, except for the bees. Warily, and with his trident at the ready, he walked across the clearing towards the house, surprised to see that it had no windows.

'My name is Amos Daragon! I would like to talk to someone!' called Amos, knocking on the door.

Still no answer. Gently, he lifted the latch and pushed open the door. Glancing around the room, Amos was struck by the strong smell of musk. The house was filled with the unmistakable scent of a wild animal. Perched on top of a stool was a little candle with a flickering flame. In the middle of the room, the remnants of a fire smouldered. Daylight filtered in through an opening in the roof where the smoke from the fireplace escaped. On a low wooden table stood a chunk of bread and a pot of honey. Next to the door, Amos saw the big sack of provisions he had witnessed being stolen from the market.

Suddenly, there was a great commotion. The table flew through the air, smashed against the wall and crashed to the floor. A tawny-coloured bear, howling with rage, leaped on Amos and, with a single swipe of his paw, sent him flying through the door. In another second the animal was on top of Amos, pinning him down with all its weight. Just as the razor-sharp claws were about to slash his face, Amos grabbed his ivory trident and aimed it at the animal's throat. The two combatants froze, each poised to kill the other. The bees had gathered in a cloud above the bear's head and were ready to join in the fight. As the bear growled orders to his flying army, Amos realized his opponent had a strange power over the bees. Fearing the worst, Amos spoke up.

'I don't want to hurt you. I want to talk to you about your parents. You're crushing me...'

He stopped. Before Amos' astonished eyes, parts of the bear's body were taking on human shape. His face was now that of the fat boy Amos had seen in the market, but he still had enormously sharp animal teeth. His right arm, raised and ready to strike, was still a bear's paw, while the arm which pinned Amos solidly to the floor was that of a human. The trident still at his throat, the manimal spoke:

'I don't trust you! I've seen you with the knights – you even live in an inn that belongs to one of them. I noticed you long before you ever saw me. You're a spy and I'm going to kill you.'

Amos thought for a moment, then dropped his weapon.

'Very well, if you must kill me, kill me! Since you know me so well, you must know that I am not from this kingdom, nor am I a threat to you. I suggest you eat me quickly. But then you'll never learn what happened to your parents.'

With a wave of his hand, the young manimal ordered the bees back to their hives. He was now fully human again. Relaxing his aggressive stance, the fat boy sank to the floor and began to sob.

'I know what the knights did. They think it was my parents who turned all the people into stone statues. But I'm no magician, and neither was my father or my mother! I won't hurt you. I'd rather you killed me instead and freed me from my pain.'

When Amos stood up again, he saw that his leather armour was slashed by four long claw marks across his chest. Without its protection, he would have been mortally wounded.

'You're incredibly strong!' he said to the fat boy. 'And since you already know this sad news, there's nothing more I can tell you. I'm sorry. If there's anything I can do for you, you only have to ask.'

The fat boy looked happier. He had stopped crying and the rage had gone from his dark eyes. With his chubby pink cheeks, long, blond sideburns and round body, he looked almost likeable. If it weren't for his sideburns, the thick eyebrows that met above his nose, and the hair that covered the palms of his hands, he would have looked like any normal boy.

'This is the first time I've ever known a human show kindness to a manimal!' he smiled. 'My name is Beorf Bromanson. There are very few people like me left in this world. I belong to the tribe of the beast-men. Legends say that manimals were the first creatures to inhabit this planet. We had our own kings who ruled magnificent kingdoms in the midst of great forests. Each family was linked, by soul and by blood, to an animal.

There were dog-men, bird-men, and many, many other creatures that could transform themselves at will. I'm from the Kingdom of Bears.

'Unfortunately, humans never trusted us and as a result many of us were killed. I've never actually met any manimals other than my parents. My father often said we might well be the last family of the Kingdom of Bears to walk the earth. I could be the last of my race.'

Since Beorf lived in the forest, it occurred to Amos that he might know something about the mysterious evil force that had done so much damage in the kingdom. He asked Beorf if he knew who, or what, was turning the villagers to stone.

'I've seen them!' Beorf said. 'It's a long story, and I'm too tired and sad to tell it now. Come and see me tomorrow and I'll tell you everything I know about those horrible creatures.'

The two boys shook hands warmly and Amos left, promising to return first thing in the morning. He hadn't walked far when knights on horseback raced by at full gallop. He turned and hurried back, just in time to see a detachment of a dozen Knights of the Light toss a net over Beorf. Transformed into a bear again, the manimal struggled to free himself from the trap. The bees swarmed around, savagely attacking the armed men. Only when Beorf was knocked unconscious did they stop fighting and return to their hives. The knights set fire to Beorf's cottage.

Inside the net, the fat boy had changed into his human form. His hands and feet were tied and he was slung across the back of a horse. Amos would have liked to come to his friend's aid, but he was wise enough to know he didn't stand a chance if he confronted these powerful warriors. Hidden in the woods, Amos watched the Knights of the Light take his new friend away, while the flames shot up from what was left of his house. Witnessing this spectacle, Amos swore he would save the manimal from being burned at the stake. He couldn't forget Beorf's words: 'Unfortunately, humans never trusted us and many of us were killed.'

Amos raced back through the forest to Great Bratel.

CHAPTER FIVE

THE GAME OF TRUTH

When Amos reached the city he was out of breath and exhausted. He made his way at once to The Arms and the Sword, where he found Barthelemy talking with three other knights. The three knights had removed their armour and were applying ointment to the dozens of bee stings that covered their skin. They had been stung everywhere – under their arms, behind their knees, inside their mouths and even on the soles of their feet.

'Those bees were devils!' exclaimed one knight loudly. 'Look, I've even been stung on my the palm of my sword-hand! How is that possible? I was holding my weapon firmly, and the damned things still managed to get in there!'

'That's nothing,' answered another. 'Look at my leg. It's swollen so much I can hardly move it. I've counted exactly fifty-three stings! But on my other leg there's nothing, not a trace of a sting. Those bees knew full well what they were doing! They certainly wanted to unhorse me – an enemy on the ground is a vanquished enemy!

'And what about me?' the third knight muttered, 'I was stung on de moush and around de eyes. I can varely shee anyshing! Bur at leasht I can shtill talk alwight!'

Amos went over to Barthelemy and asked to speak with him immediately, in private. They went to a corner away from the other knights.

'You've made a mistake by capturing that young manimal from the forest! He has nothing to do with what's going on, in fact he's the only one who has information about our enemies. You have to release him!'

Barthelemy seemed surprised.

'How do you know all this, Amos? In any case, there's nothing I can do. Tomorrow at dawn he will be burned at the stake.'

'We must save him,' Amos insisted. 'If you can't do anything, who else can I approach to beg for his freedom?'

'Only Yaune the Purifier, my young friend,' declared the knight. 'It was he who ordered that anyone practising magic should be burned. The knights obey their master and never question his decisions. Manimals are treacherous creatures that deserve to be put to death. Tonight, you can go to the boy's trial, but I advise you not to defend him. You could end up sharing his fate.'

Amos asked Barthelemy what this so-called trial would involve, since it was obvious that Beorf's fate was already sealed.

'The manimal will be subjected to the Game of Truth. Yaune places two pieces of paper inside his helmet. One has the word 'guilty' written on it, and the other, the word 'innocent'. The accused draws a paper at random, and that choice determines his guilt or innocence. I have never seen a single accused person draw the paper that says 'innocent.' Yaune the Purifier is never wrong. If your friend is innocent, the truth will shine in the light of day and he will be saved. But it would be the first time in the entire history of the Knights of the Light that such a thing had happened!'

Awaiting Beorf's trial, Amos walked through the streets of the city. The market square had been transformed into a courtroom and his friend was now a prisoner in a cage, exposed to the glares and insults of passers-by. Many threw rotten tomatoes and eggs at him. Beorf hung his head and fumed in silence. When their eyes met, Amos could read the hatred and contempt in his friend's face.

And why should he feel otherwise, thought Amos. Why did the ignorance of human beings always lead them to imprison the innocent, to publicly humiliate them and threaten them with death? Beorf could be burned at the stake! Just like his parents, he might well be condemned without any proof. And did any of the self-satisfied people in this square, who were salivating at the thought of the impending spectacle, feel the slightest twinge of compassion? Hadn't this city, under the pretext of protecting itself, murdered enough innocents? No, they needed another, then perhaps another and even another to quench their thirst for blood. All those knights thought they were doing good and never questioned their actions, but not one could see beyond the end of his nose! Amos suddenly felt sick. He ducked behind the crumbling wall of an abandoned house, his stomach churning.

A large crowd was gathering in the square. Amos paced back and forth, racking his brains for a solution. He had to save his new friend, but how? Somehow Amos had the feeling this Game of Truth was merely a trick used by Yaune the Purifier to validate his decisions so no one dared to challenge them. But how did he do it?

Amos picked up two stones, the same size but different colours, and put them in his pocket. The darker stone would represent 'guilty'; the pale grey one 'innocent'. Pulling out a stone at random, Amos found he had chosen the light-coloured stone six times out of ten and the darker stone four times. He did it over and over again. The result was always more or less the same. He was never able to pick the same stone ten times in a row. So it was impossible that Yaune's Game of Truth could be fair! From what Barthelemy had said, there had been many trials in the kingdom and never had a single accused person won his or her freedom in the Game of Truth. Everyone had been proven guilty – a fact that defied all logic!

Suddenly, it all became clear. If the word 'guilty' was picked every time, this could only mean that the word was written on both pieces of paper. It was impossible to pick a piece of paper with 'innocent' on it, because it didn't exist! Yaune was a fraud, a liar and a cheat. With these ideas whirling around in his head, Amos racked his brain for a way to foil Yaune's dishonest trick and free Beorf.

But the trial was about to begin and he still hadn't found a solution. Only when he threw the dark stone on the ground and kept the lighter stone in his pocket did the answer come to him. It was so obvious! He started to laugh. He had finally found the trick that could free his friend.

The tall figure of Yaune the Purifier strode across the platform. He was about sixty years old, with long salt-and-pepper-coloured hair and a bushy grey beard.

A scar extended from his right eye down to his upper lip. His fine gold armour glistened in the sun. His helmet was decorated with two white wings and around his neck he wore a thick chain from which hung a heavy pendant. It looked like a skull sculpted from a green stone, and it had eyes which shone like two huge diamonds. Yaune was as dignified and solid as an oak tree, and his solemn expression commanded respect.

The crowd was agitated. The gates of Great Bratel had already been closed for the night, and all the knights were present at the trial. To thunderous applause, Yaune the Purifier rose to speak:

'We are here so the light may triumph once again. Inhabitants of Great Bratel, the boy you see before you in this cage is a wizard. Several knights witnessed his transformation into an animal. A knight never lies, and the word of my men must never be questioned. This wizard's magic is powerful and, like the others we have captured, he will be condemned to purification by fire, so our kingdom may be saved from the threat that hangs over our heads. Unless, of course, the Game of Truth reveals his innocence. It is only by eliminating all forms of magic that we will be able to vanquish the evil that threatens us. The truth and the light are our guides. So far, our intuitions have been sound and our actions heroic. Let anyone who doubts the guilt of this young wizard now come forth, or forever hold his peace!'

A deep hush fell over the assembly. Amos raised his hand and, in a voice that betrayed his nervousness, called:

'I know you are making a mistake!'

All eyes fell on this boy who, before the whole court, dared to call into question the word of Yaune and his knights.

'Silence, young man!' Yaune shot back sternly. 'Your impertinence can be excused by your youth and lack of experience. Now, withdraw your words or you will suffer the consequences!'

'I withdraw nothing of what I have just said, my lord,' Amos replied, growing in confidence. 'This boy is named Beorf and he is my friend. He is of the race of manimals. He is not a magician, and certainly not a creature that transforms men into stone statues. He is innocent of the crimes for which he stands accused. If you burn him, you will never know what is really happening in your kingdom because he is the only one who has seen the creatures that threaten you!'

For the first time in his reign, someone was challenging Yaune the Purifier.

'Do you think, you little scoundrel, that you are wiser than the Lord of Great Bratel? For almost forty years I have fought the dark forces of this world. I have shed my blood in the name of truth. I have lost men, and entire armies – all so that the light of man can triumph over the dark, evil world that lurks behind the shadows. Approach the platform so I can get a better look at you.'

Amos walked forward in silent dignity. Yaune smiled when he saw the young lad with his long, braided hair, his torn leather armour and the trident slung across his back. Barthelemy stepped forward. He fell to his knees before his lord and spoke to him in a low voice:

'Forgive him, great lord. This child is a fool. He has no idea what he is saying. I know him, he lives with his parents at my mother's inn. They are travellers who recently arrived here. His father and mother know nothing of what he is doing. Please forgive this child. I will vouch for him.'

Yaune was mollified.

'Very well, valiant Barthelemy. Your father saved my life many times, and I owe his descendants the same respect I had for him. Take this boy away and don't let me ever see him again in Great Bratel.'

Just then, a man stepped out of the crowd.

'Lord Yaune, my name is Urban Daragon! I know my son better than the knight Barthelemy and I can assure you that if Amos says your prisoner is innocent, it's because he is speaking the truth. Barthelemy is a good man and I understand that he wants to protect the travellers he has befriended. The Daragon family thank him with all our hearts, but I have always taught my son to act according to his deepest convictions. Amos is not a fool, and your people would benefit from hearing what he has to say.'

Impatiently, Yaune dismissed Barthelemy with a wave of his hand and declared with a sigh:

'May the will of the father be done! And we will see that justice is done. I will subject this boy to the Game of Truth. We will play for the fate of the young wizard prisoner. I will put two pieces of paper in my helmet. One, as you know, bears the word 'guilty' and the other, the word 'innocent.' You, my impudent young friend, will select a piece of paper at random. If you pick the paper that says 'innocent,' I will spare the life of your friend the wizard. If, on the other hand, you pick the paper with the word 'guilty,' we will have three people to burn at the stake – the young wizard, your father and yourself. All who undertake to defend the enemies of Yaune the Purifier are traitors and deserve to die! This will teach your father that it is sometimes better to obey the law of the kingdom rather than his own personal convictions. Bring me two pieces of paper and we will proceed!'

While Yaune was writing on the papers, Amos gave Beorf a quick wink and smiled.

'I submit to the laws of this kingdom,' he said, 'and I will gladly play the Game of Truth. Just let me see what you have written on the two pieces of paper before you put them into your helmet.'

Yaune was taken aback by this request, but quickly regained his composure.

'Enough of your nonsense! I am a knight, I cannot lie or cheat. Step onto the platform, and may the truth illuminate all our lives!'

But the lord of Great Bratel was uneasy, and this reassured Amos. He must have written 'guilty' on both pieces of paper – Amos could read it in his eyes. Urban Daragon was sweating profusely and hoping against hope that his son had a trick up his sleeve that would keep them from the stake. Barthelemy watched nervously, certain that when the sun rose again, he would be watching his new friends in flames. Beorf was panting. He could not believe that Amos would risk his own life and that of his father to save him, a manimal despised by all humans. The crowd, certain of the outcome, remained calm. Their lord was never wrong. No one doubted that next day there would be a huge bonfire in Great Bratel.

Calmly, Amos reached into the helmet. Then, swiftly, he took the piece of paper, popped it into his mouth and swallowed it in one gulp.

'What are you doing, you little fool?' growled Yaune.

'Simple: I took the piece of paper and I ate it.' Amos declared, smiling.

Some of the spectators began giggling, but Yaune fumed with rage.

'You little idiot, why did you do that?' he shouted.

'Since I ate the paper I picked at random, we still don't know if my friend is innocent or guilty,' Amos answered solemnly. 'But to find out, we just have to look at the paper that's still in the helmet. If it says "innocent", then I must have picked and eaten the one marked "guilty", and you will burn us tomorrow morning at dawn. If, on the other hand, we find the word "guilty", it means I ate the paper that said "innocent". And that will be our salvation! Now, I would like Barthelemy to come and read the verdict.'

The knight came forward, took the paper from the helmet and called out loud and clear:

'Guilty!'

'That proves that the paper I chose first said "innocent",' said Amos, triumphantly. 'Unless, of course, both pieces of paper in the helmet said "guilty" – and I know that the leader of the Knights of the Light is not a cheat. Therefore, the truth has spoken!'

The crowd burst into applause. Yaune leapt to his feet, his face scarlet with rage.

'The truth has spoken,' he declared. 'Free the boy from his cage.'

Then he whispered in Amos' ear:

'I will make you pay dearly for this trick. You'll learn that nobody crosses the Lord of Great Bratel and gets away with it.'

CHAPTER SIX

THROWN OUT OF GREAT BRATEL

A bright, round moon threw a soft light over Great Bratel as Amos returned to the inn with his father and Beorf. The Daragons welcomed the young manimal like a son and during supper Amos explained how he had met Beorf in the forest. He also told them how the knights had captured his father and mother and burned them at the stake.

This worried Frilla, who wanted to leave Great Bratel as soon as possible. She reminded them that their real goal was to reach Tarkasis Forest. Spending more time at the inn – especially in a city where the knights were ready to burn anyone at the drop of a hat – was not such a good idea. They still had money in their purse and the horses were well rested. They decided to leave at dawn and take Beorf with them.

Beorf had just started to tell them what he had seen in the forest when he stopped abruptly, staring at the cat the family had rescued.

'Don't worry, he's not dangerous,' Amos said, smiling. 'He's blind. We found him in a village on our way here. He was the only living creature we came across – all the people and animals were transformed into statues. We took pity on him and brought him with us.'

Beorf whistled to get the cat's attention and then threw him a piece of meat from his plate. The cat immediately sprang up and caught it.

'That animal isn't blind, you can see for yourselves! Never trust appearances. And beware of that cat – it isn't normal. There's something about it I don't like. I can tune in to that kind of thing with animals, I can sense their evil intentions. It's hiding its game very well, pretending to be blind, but it's watching us and listening to us, too.'

To reassure him, Frilla Daragon picked up the cat and took it upstairs to her bedroom. Before setting it down on the bed, she looked closely into the animal's eyes. It really was blind. Two thick cataracts covered its eyes. This convinced her that the young manimal was mistaken and, feeling better, she returned to take her seat at the table. Beorf continued the tale of what he had seen in the forest.

'They were women, with monstrous, powerful bodies, wings on their backs and long claws on their feet. They had greenish skin and massive, round heads, with flat noses and protruding teeth like wild boars. They had forked tongues that hung down to one side, and their eyes blazed. When I first saw them, I wondered why their hair was moving all the time. I almost died of fright when I realized it wasn't hair, but dozens and dozens of writhing snakes! These evil creatures come out at night. They scream constantly because the snakes attack them and bite their shoulders and backs. A thick, black, sticky liquid oozes from the wounds. As soon as any living being looks into their eyes, they are immediately turned to stone!'

Amos interrupted him. 'But how can you know that they have a blazing glow in their eyes if everyone who looks at them is transformed into a statue? Why weren't you petrified, too?'

Beorf was taken aback by this. He should indeed have met the same fate as the others. Why hadn't he? But then he remembered exactly what had happened.

'I was looking for wild fruit near a little village when nightfall took me by surprise. I fell asleep in the warm grass and was wakened by the villagers screaming in panic. In bear form, I ventured closer to the houses to see what the commotion was all about. I hid behind the blacksmith's forge and watched through a hole in the wall, but I couldn't see much from there. It was then that I saw a large mirror inside the forge. The knights must have used it when they were trying on new suits of armour – the Knights of the Light are so vain and full of themselves! If they could, they'd ride with mirrors in front of them at all times, to admire themselves. Anyway, thanks to the mirror, I was able to get a clear look at the creatures. That's how I managed see their eyes without being turned to stone. I realize now that I was lucky to escape with my life!'

'Now we know what the creatures look like,' said Frilla. 'But what do they want and why are they attacking this city?'

'Well, at least we know how to avoid being turned into statues,' Amos yawned. 'Besides, it's obvious that...'

'Shh! Quiet!' whispered Beorf, grabbing his arm. 'Look discreetly at the beam above you. Your blind cat is spying on us.'

The whole family looked up at the same time. The cat was indeed there, just above the table, and it appeared to be listening in on their conversation.

'You see, I was right,' said Beorf. 'Its ears are far too big and its eyes are far too round to be an ordinary domestic cat. As soon as it comes down from its perch, it'll get what's coming to it! That little snoop is working for those creatures – I'm sure of it.'

Just at that moment, Barthelemy, followed by five other knights, burst into the inn. They strode over to the Daragons' table.

'By order of Yaune the Purifier, Lord of Great Bratel,' declared Barthelemy, 'we must expel Amos

Daragon and his friend Beorf from the city.'

'I'm sorry,' he added, 'to have to do such a thing, but I must obey orders. Knights, take them away!'

Urban leaped up to stop the soldiers laying hands on his son. A hard blow to the back of his head knocked him unconscious. Frilla begged Barthelemy not to take her son away – outside the city walls, Amos would be easy prey for the creatures. But it was no use. Barthelemy was deaf to her pleas. Beorf was all for changing into a bear and selling his skin at the highest price, but Amos managed to stop him. As the knights left the inn with their prisoners, the cat jumped down onto the window ledge and, quick as lightning, slipped through a broken window-pane and into the night.

The two huge wooden gates creaked open and the portcullis was raised. Once the knights had marched them out and closed the gates behind them, Amos and Beorf found themselves alone and completely defenceless outside the city walls.

'We must think, my friend,' said Amos. 'We need a hiding place! I don't know the fields around this city at all, much less the forest. You have to get us out of here before the creatures with the snake-hair get their claws into us!'

'I know where we can go,' said Beorf. 'Climb on my back – and hang on tight!'

With this, the manimal transformed into a bear. Amos jumped onto his back and gripped his fur tightly. In an instant they were off, running swiftly. In spite of the darkness, Beorf knew the surroundings well and found his way without difficulty. Eventually they came to the foot of a gigantic tree. Beorf, once again in human form, was sweating profusely. He lay on his back, his fat belly heaving up and down. It took him a few minutes to catch his breath.

'Quick! Let's... let's get down there!' he gasped finally.

Digging with his hands, Beorf uncovered and opened a trap door. A ladder led underground, directly beneath the tree. When they reached the bottom they found themselves in total darkness. Beorf groped about for a lamp. When he found it, he said:

'Watch closely, Amos, I'm going to do some magic!'

He muttered something softly, then a kind of growl rose from deep inside his chest. Amos looked up to see a swarm of little lights fly in through the open trap door. Within seconds, dozens and then hundreds of fireflies were hovering above them. Suddenly the insects swooped down around Beorf and gathered inside the big glass lamp in his hand. As light filled the underground room, it revealed a library.

All four walls were lined with books. Big ones, small ones – there were books everywhere. In the middle of the room was a large desk with a comfortable chair. In one corner, a pile of straw and blankets was arranged as a bed. Beorf climbed the ladder to close the trap door.

'This hiding place is safe,' he said. 'Nobody will find us here. Welcome to my father's den. He had a passion for reading and studied all the time. There are books here on every subject. My father had them sent from far and wide. Many are written in strange languages I can't understand. Have a look at them, if you like. I'm going to bed – I'm exhausted. To turn off the fireflies, just grunt three times. Good night, Amos.'

Beorf's head had barely touched the pillow when he starting snoring. Amos walked around the room looking at the books. There must have been at least a thousand. Some were old and dusty, while others appeared to be quite recent. Amos noticed one book that had not been put back on the shelf. It was an old volume, transcribed by hand and entitled: *Al-Qatrum, the Territories of the Netherworld*. He picked it up, sat down at Beorf's father's desk and began to read.

The book described a land beyond the far limit of Hyperborea. It was a world hidden in the bowels of the earth, where the sun never shone. This land was the haunt of creatures of the night, the birthplace of hosts of monsters that had then spread across the Earth.

To his great surprise, Amos came across a drawing depicting the creatures Beorf had described at the inn. They were known as 'gorgons', and their origins seemed to date far back. Once, a beautiful young princess called Medusa reigned over an island in the great sea of Hyperborea. Her beauty was such that Phorcys, the

God of the Waters, fell madly in love with her. Ceto, Phorcys' sister, wanting desperately to keep her brother's love for herself, transformed Medusa into a hideous, dangerous creature. To make sure that Phorcys would never again look into Medusa's eyes, Ceto gave her the power to change any living being that did so into stone. Princess Medusa also received the poisoned gift of immortality, and was condemned to endure her ugliness for century after century. Every time one of her hair-snakes bit her, the drops of blood that fell to the ground turned into snakes. After many long years, each snake became another gorgon. Apparently, the island of the beautiful Princess Medusa still existed and was populated by stone statues.

Amos closed the book. Now he knew the history of the monsters, he needed to find out why they were attacking the kingdom of the Knights of the Light. Beorf's father must have been trying to unravel the mystery before his death. This book had probably been left off the shelf because he'd been consulting it recently. Looking in the desk drawer, Amos found a pile of Mr. Bromanson's notes. Among them was a drawing that looked familiar. It was the skull pendant that hung around the neck of Yaune the Purifier! Amos read on.

According to Beorf's father, Yaune the Purifier had stolen the sacred relic in his youth. In those days he was known as Yaune the Odious. In a far-off land, he and his army had attacked a village populated with witches and wizards, and stolen this black-magic symbol from a holy temple. The owner of the pendant, a cruel magician, had been searching for it ever since. Only one man of the army of the Knights of the Light had returned safe and sound to Great Bratel. Claiming that he had eliminated all his enemies, Yaune the Odious had been given the name of Yaune the Purifier and had been proclaimed lord and master of the city.

'That explains everything,' thought Amos. 'That must have been the battle in which Barthelemy's father was killed. The gorgons serve this dark magician, and until he gets his pendant back, the city and the surrounding region will be in danger. Now I understand why Yaune burns all the magicians who are captured by his knights. He's afraid, and he knows he's no match for that dark wizard.'

Suddenly, Amos had the feeling he was being watched. There in front of him, in the shadow of the passageway leading to the trap door, sat the blind cat. At once, the animal backed away, disappearing into the shadows.

CHAPTER SEVEN

THE DRUID

mos' sleep was troubled. Thoughts of the gorgons, the pendant, Yaune and the cat were milling around in his head, and his mind swarmed with dark images. He awoke to find that Beorf had served breakfast on his father's desk. A soft light poured into the library through a round window in the ceiling. Amos couldn't believe his eyes. There was honey, nuts, wild fruit, bread, milk and cakes.

'Where did you get all this?' he asked his friend.

'Oh, I have my hiding places,' Beorf answered, swallowing a big slice of bread dripping with honey.

Amos enjoyed that first meal of the day with his friend. He told Beorf everything he had discovered about his father's research. He then told him all about his adventure in the Bay of Caves, his departure from the Kingdom of Omain, and his journey with his parents to Great Bratel. Then Amos took the mermaid's white stone from a little bag that he kept inside his armour and set it down on the table.

'Look. I have to go to Tarkasis Forest to give this stone to Gwenfadrilla. I must tell her that her friend Crivannia, Princess of the Waters, is dead, and her kingdom has fallen into the hands of the merrows. She also needs to know that I was chosen by Crivannia to be a mask wearer. If only I knew what all this meant! It's a complete mystery to me...'

Just as Amos was finishing his sentence, the blind cat jumped down from a shelf and landed on the table. Seizing the white stone in its teeth, it sprang for the trap door.

'I'll have your hide, you filthy beast!' Beorf shouted. His voice was loud and gruff. In his bear form he bounded after the cat, which climbed nimbly up the ladder and slipped out through the trap door. Beorf slipped twice trying to scale the rungs, but on the third try, he made it up the ladder. Amos quickly grabbed his things. Tucking the book *Al-Qatrum, The Territories of the Netherworld* under his arm and slinging the trident across his back, he ran for the ladder.

Once outside, he followed Beorf's tracks. The trail led straight to Great Bratel, and Amos was astonished to see that, in spite of the late hour, the portcullis protecting the city gates was still open. There were no peasants working in the fields. In a flash, Amos realized what must have happened and as he entered the capital, his worst fears were confirmed. All the inhabitants had been transformed into stone statues. Nobody, it seemed, had escaped the spell.

As Amos ran to The Arms and the Sword, he encountered only stone statues, their faces etched with fear. At the door of the Inn, Barthelemy stood motionless, a pitiful sight. Amos looked around in vain for his parents. He clung to the hope that he would find them safe and sound. After all, Urban and Frilla knew the powers of the gorgons and may have fled in time. It was the cries of a panicked bear coming from the centre of the city that brought his mind back to Beorf. Amos ran as fast as he could to the market square.

The manimal was being held prisoner by strong roots, which had wrapped themselves around his paws, body and throat. Amos was amazed. How could roots have grown fast enough to completely immobilize a powerful creature like Beorf? Grabbing his trident, Amos tried to free the bear, but was suddenly stopped by the voice of a man.

'It's useless, Master Daragon, to try to free your friend. The strength of a root is equal to the power of the druid who made it grow. I don't mean to brag, but I can assure you that a dozen woodcutters armed with heavy axes couldn't cut through these roots.'

Amos nervously pointed his weapon at the old man whose chin was hidden beneath a long, dirty, grey beard. His hair was long and horribly tangled; bits of twig, leaves, and grass stuck out here and there. He wore a brown robe that was stained and full of holes, a braid of vines as a belt, and wooden shoes. A long, twisted staff completed his outfit. His hands were covered with the kind of moss normally seen on rocks, and a huge red mushroom grew out of his neck. At the old man's feet was the blind cat, rubbing its head against his legs.

'Stop threatening me with that weapon, young man! You're scaring me! Oh! How you're scaring me!' said the old druid, laughing. 'Let's talk for a minute. I must know if you are worthy of the confidence that Crivannia showed you before she died.'

But Amos wasn't listening.

'Your cat stole my white stone and I want it back. Right now!'

The old man, surprised by the boy's confidence, replied:

'Oh, Master Daragon is making demands, is he? He's giving me orders and threatening me with his ivory trident! True, it's a dangerous weapon, but since you don't seem to know how to use it properly, I hardly fear for my life.'

The druid opened his hand and Amos could see the white stone partly concealed between his dirty fingers.

'You know my cat, I believe. I have been observing you through his eyes for quite some time. You're very clever, my dear child. I can sense your question: why can this animal sometimes see and sometimes not? That's a good question, Master Daragon, and I will answer it. When I look through his eyes, he ceases to be blind. It's as simple as that. Any more questions? Yes? Am I the dark magician who seeks his pendant and controls the army of gorgons? No, Master Daragon. As I told you, I am a druid – a rather dirty druid, I must admit. A druid who doesn't always smell very good, I'll give you that too, but I am not evil and I work for neither the forces of darkness nor the forces of light. Well, you'll understand later… Oh no! You have another question? What am I doing here, at the centre of a city populated with statues, holding your white stone in my hand? Patience, we're coming to that! But now it's your turn to answer my questions. I want to know if you're intelligent enough to become a mask wearer.'

'Free Beorf first,' Amos demanded. 'Then I'll answer all your questions.'

The druid smiled. Half his yellow teeth were rotten and loose. With a twitch of his nose, the old man withdrew his spell. The roots that had imprisoned Beorf dropped limply to the ground and shrivelled up.

'Now, think fast, my young friend,' said the old man. 'What can be thrown over a house once, but not twice?'

'That's simple!' Amos answered. 'An egg. Someone

could throw it once over a house pretty easily, but after landing it could hardly be thrown again.'

The old man looked surprised at hearing the correct answer.

'That was an easy one. Now we'll have something more complicated. What creature can go over a house but can't cross a little stream of water?'

'You think that's harder?' Amos asked, chuckling. 'I think it's much simpler than the first one. It's an ant, of course.'

The druid was beginning to get flustered. He'd never met anyone with such a quick mind.

'Good luck with this one, boy. What goes around wood, but never goes into it?'

'Bark, of course' answered Amos, sighing with exasperation. 'Far too easy!'

'Alright, this is my best one! Listen carefully,' continued the druid, certain that his next question was a killer. 'What makes shadows in the woods without ever being in the woods?'

Amos laughed.

'It's the sun that makes shadows in the woods without ever being in the woods! Now, if you think you're so clever, answer me this. The more you add, the less it weighs. What is it?'

The druid thought for a moment.

'I don't know,' he admitted. 'What is it?'

'I'll tell you after you tell me what you're doing here.'

'Do you promise to tell me, Master Daragon?' asked the druid anxiously.

'My word is my truth!' Amos replied.

'Very well. Very well. I will try to explain, although it's rather complicated. I came here to investigate the events of recent weeks, and to look into the matter of Yaune the Purifier and the pendant. Your reading yesterday helped me a great deal. Through the eyes of my cat, I was able to read the same things as you. My druidic order believes that the pendant is dangerous and must under no circumstances fall into the wrong hands. That is why, during the night, when Yaune and his army were transformed into statues, I stole his pendant so the gorgons could not return it to their master. You see, Master Daragon, I am a powerful druid, but I must not in any way become directly involved in this matter. I am a magician in the realm of nature, not a mask wearer. I protect animals and plants. I do not protect people.

'There are two forces in this world that are constantly at odds, namely good and evil. They are what we call the forces of light and the forces of darkness. Ever since the beginning of time, since the sun and moon have shared the earth, these two powers have been constantly playing out their battle through human beings. The mask wearers are humans, chosen for their spiritual and intellectual qualities. Their mission is to re-establish the balance between day and night, between good and evil. Since it is impossible to get rid of either the sun or the moon, they must be kept in equal balance. Mask wearers have been extinct in this world for many centuries. If Crivannia has chosen you, it is because she wants to make you the first of a new generation of warriors. Your task is to restore balance to this world.

'A great war is brewing. The merrows are already attacking the mermaids, and soon they will take over the oceans. Go quickly to Tarkasis Forest. I am returning your stone to you and entrusting you with Yaune the Purifier's pendant. It is up to you to decide if it should be returned to its owner. That is your task, not mine. We will no doubt meet again. And now, I would like the answer to your riddle. The more you add, the less it weighs: what is it?'

'I'll tell you. But first, explain to me what a "mask wearer" is,' said Amos.

'I cannot answer you, Master Daragon,' replied the druid wearily. 'Tell me, I need to know! The more you add, the less it weighs? What is it?'

'Holes in a plank of wood,' answered the boy, with a straight face.

The old man roared with laughter, slapping his sides.

'Oh, that's a good one! Better than any of mine! I should have thought of that! Holes in a plank of wood! Obviously, the more you add the less it weighs! Here, take the pendant and the stone! That really is a good one! Really, really good! Now, goodbye and good luck! My cat will keep an eye out for you! Holes in a...'

Still laughing, the druid walked towards one of the big trees in the square and disappeared straight through the trunk. Beorf, once again in human form, put an arm around Amos' neck and rubbed the pendant with the tip of his index finger.

'I think we're in a fine pickle, my friend' he said.

Amos felt completely overwhelmed. He had absolutely no idea what to do next.

'It's hopeless, Beorf. I don't know what to do with this stone. And I don't know what to do with this horrible pendant! My parents have disappeared and I have no idea where they are. I was chosen as a mask wearer and I have no idea what that means. According to the druid, my ivory trident is a powerful weapon that I don't know how to use properly. Soon, an army of gorgons led by an angry dark magician will be hot on our heels. We're in the middle of a capital city populated by statues, and I'm absolutely certain that the creatures responsible for that will return tonight to search the city. And how am I supposed to re-establish the balance between good and evil? Is there a way to break the evil spell and bring all the people back to life? They've paid a high price for the theft of this pendant and they don't deserve to remain statues for eternity. But I haven't a clue where to begin

– I have no idea how to get us out of this jam.'

'Alright, let's just think for a minute and try to analyse the situation calmly,' said Beorf. 'Your first mission is to go to Tarkasis Forest. That's what you should do before you do anything else. But if you take the pendant with you, the gorgons will follow you and all the villages you pass through will fall under their spell. I think the gorgons can sense its presence and its power. We could try to destroy the pendant, but it might hold power that could be useful to us.

'The dark magician came here to find his pendant and he must not leave this area. I'll make sure that I leave clues as to my movements and particularly the whereabouts of the pendant. That way, the magician will stay within the kingdom. We have to find out who he is, where he's hiding and how we can get rid of him. We'd better split up. I'll stay here with the pendant. I know the meadows and forest around here very well; I'll hide where the gorgons will never find me. I'll look after the pendant while you try to find out more about the white stone, your trident, and your mission. Go on now – if you're quick you can get out of the kingdom before nightfall. Trust me, this is the best solution.'

Amos did not want to leave his friend and face the danger alone. He tried to convince him they should try to find some other way, but Beorf's mind was made up. It was clearly the most logical course of action. Handing the pendant over to Beorf, Amos made his way to The

Arms and the Sword to get his things. All the horses had been petrified, so he would have to set out on his journey on foot.

'This is it, Beorf. I'm leaving. Take care of yourself, my friend.'

The manimal smiled. Then, transforming his right hand into a bear's paw, he showed Amos his long, sharp claws.

'Just leave the gorgons to me!' he said.

CHAPTER EIGHT

THE OLD WOMAN'S EGG

It was now almost two weeks since Amos had left Great Bratel. The journey had been long and difficult. Not knowing where Tarkasis Forest was, he had to stop many people to ask for directions. Most of the people he asked had never heard the name, or if they had, it was only in stories and legends. Puzzled, Amos wandered from village to village. Sometimes he joined a merchant caravan or a group of troubadours, who paid little heed to his questions. Most of the time, he travelled alone.

Amos found food by scavenging in the woods, or by bartering a day of work in the fields for a meal and a bed for the night. Most nights he slept in the forest beside roads seldom travelled. As the days passed, he grew more and more anxious, regretting that his friend Beorf was not with him. He often wondered if he had made the wrong decision in leaving Great Bratel alone.

Almost everywhere he heard disturbing rumours that the Knights of the Light had fallen under a terrible evil spell and that their kingdom was to be avoided at all costs. Villagers were suspicious and did not welcome strangers. Amos even heard rumours about himself, warning people to be wary of a boy of about ten who, suspiciously, was travelling without his parents. When they met him, people asked him all kinds of questions, simply because they were wary of his intentions.

Amos' only distraction during his long journey to Tarkasis Forest was the book he had taken from Beorf's father's library. *Al-Qatrum, the Territories of the Netherworld* was a virtual encyclopaedia of all the evil creatures of the night. There were maps, drawings and a great deal of information about the most frightful monsters.

It was from this book that Amos discovered the existence of a creature called the basilisk. The impressive illustration showed a creature with the body and tail of a serpent, and the wings and feet of a cockerel. Its head was crested and its beak was that of a vulture. Described as one of the most horrible and terrifying creatures ever to walk the earth, the basilisk was the creation of a dark magician. To bring a basilisk to life, one had to find a cockerel's egg and have it hatched by a toad for at least one day. This would produce a monster that, with its hiss alone, could paralyse its victim before attacking.

The basilisk always bit its victim in the same place, in

the soft flesh on the nape of the neck. The poisonous bite was always fatal, for no antidote had ever been discovered. And according to the book, just the gaze of a basilisk was enough to wilt the vegetation around it and roast a bird in mid-flight. No bigger than a chicken, as agile as a snake, and as voracious as a vulture, the basilisk killed for sheer pleasure. Humans were its favourite prey, and the author of the book even noted several cities that had been completely wiped out by as few as three or four of the creatures.

Under certain conditions, however, this terrible creature was highly vulnerable. It died instantly, for example, if it heard the cock-a-doodle-doo of a cockerel. Also, like the gorgons, the basilisk could not survive seeing its own reflection. It therefore lived in constant fear of mirrors and other reflective surfaces.

The pieces of the puzzle were starting to fall into place. In Amos' mind, a solution for freeing Great Bratel from the snake-haired creatures was taking shape. First, he knew the gorgons would never leave the city without recovering the pendant. Yaune the Purifier, who knew the gorgons' powers and who should have been able to protect his men, had made a serious error. The well-polished suits of armour worn by the Knights of the Light would have acted as mirrors, so the gorgons ought to have perished instantly on meeting the knights, before they had a chance to cast their spell on the city. But Yaune had neglected one important detail. The gorgons always attacked at night, when it was too dark for the armour to reflect anything.

The only way to eliminate all the monsters at the same time would be to set up mirrors all over the city and light a thousand fires all at once! But how could such a plan be carried out? There were Beorf's fireflies, of course, but they would need millions of them.

Still working out a way to eliminate the gorgons, Amos arrived at a village and stopped to drink from a fountain. Nearby, an old woman dressed in white from head to foot was bent over her cane.

'Who are you, young man, and what are you doing here?' she said to Amos.

'I have to get to Tarkasis Forest but I don't know the area. Could you help me, please?'

The old woman looked thoughtful for a moment.

'I can't help you, I'm afraid. But you're the second person in two days who's asked me about the forest. Strange, isn't it?'

'Who did you see? Who asked you?' asked Amos, intrigued.

'A very kind gentleman and his wife. They also asked if I had seen a boy with long black hair, wearing leather armour and an earring, and carrying a long ivory staff on his back. Yesterday I hadn't seen him, but today I could swear that he's standing right before me!'

'They were my parents!' Amos exclaimed, dizzy with joy at finally hearing news of them. 'We got separated and I really need to find them again. Please, madam, tell me which way they went.'

'I believe they took that road.'

Amos thanked her profusely and was about to hurry on his way when the old woman motioned him to sit down beside her.

'I'm going to tell you something, my young friend. I know you want to dash off and find your parents as quickly as possible, but I must tell you about a dream I had last night. In my dream I was baking bread rolls. Everyone in my family had gathered around me, and I was doing my best to satisfy them. But my children, my grandchildren, my cousins, and my nephews had all been turned to stone. In my house, there was nothing but statues. Then you suddenly appeared in my dream. I didn't know you but you asked me for something to eat and I gave you three or four rolls. Biting into one of them, you found a hard-boiled egg, and I said to you: "You often find eggs where you least expect them." That's all. But since I believe that every dream has a purpose, I baked rolls this morning and brought them with me. I also have a few eggs. I'll give them to you and wish you luck in finding your parents.'

Amos didn't really understand the old woman's dream, but he thanked her, took the food and set out again. When he turned round to say a last farewell, the old lady had already disappeared.

Suddenly, it dawned on Amos. He thought about what the woman had said: 'You often find eggs where you least expect it.' The pendant that Yaune the Purifier had stolen many years ago must contain a cockerel's egg! That was why the dark magician wanted it back so badly! The pendant itself had no magical or demonic power, and represented no danger to anyone. It was simply a container to protect the egg. The magician who first owned the pendant must have wanted to create a basilisk. It was perfectly logical that the leader of an army of gorgons would want to have at his command a powerful monster that could annihilate a whole regiment with the blink of an eye.

Amos realized that the enemy of Great Bratel probably had power over all creatures even remotely related to snakes. He must be evil, treacherous and very, very dangerous. So Beorf was in great peril! How could Amos possibly warn his friend?

CHAPTER NINE

BEORF, THE GORGONS, AND THE NAGAS

O nce again, the gorgons were hot on Beorf's trail. The manimal ran through the forest with his head down, trying to avoid all the obstacles hidden by darkness. The first two days after Amos had left were fairly peaceful, since the gorgons were concentrating their search in the city. In his hiding place deep in the woods, Beorf had rested and slept a great deal in preparation for the difficult nights ahead. He had also thought long and hard about ways to defend himself against invaders. The best plan, he thought, was to pick off the gorgons one at a time.

Beorf set traps throughout the forest. He guessed that after a few nights of fruitless searching in Great Bratel, the monsters would start combing the countryside. The gorgons would then find human tracks – his – and follow them. So all over the meadows and the forest he left clear trails of footprints leading straight to his traps. To hide his real tracks the fat boy took on his bear form to set the traps. The gorgons were looking for a human thief, he thought, not a bear! They would never suspect the animal and the human tracks were one and the same.

The first night, Beorf's tracks led three gorgons straight into quicksand. Well hidden, the manimal watched by the light of the moon as they disappeared below its surface.

'That's three less!' he exclaimed.

Another group ended up in the clearing near the beehives surrounding his old house. When Beorf ordered the bees to attack, they formed a huge cloud above the gorgons and swooped down at full speed. The gorgons looked up. Petrified in mid-flight by the monsters' gaze, the bees fell from the sky like a hail of stones and cut through the gorgons' bodies. By sacrificing his bees, Beorf got rid of five more gorgons.

Beorf soon realized that although the gorgons had wings, they could not fly. So he devised another trap. The farmland around the city was criss-crossed by ditches which, when the dykes were opened, filled with water to irrigate the fields. Beorf dug several deep pits and covered them with branches and grass. The next night, eight gorgons fell into the traps, and when Beorf opened the dykes, the water flooded into the holes and drowned them all.

Tonight, though, the trap was different. Beorf had created a forest of blades, made from weapons he found in the knights' armoury. He stuck lances into the ground and hung daggers and swords from the branches of trees. There was only one route through the branches that would avoid the deadly blades. Beorf had spent the day practising dodging the blades. Now, the moment of truth was at hand.

Beorf could hear the gorgons approaching. He could not run very fast on two legs, and he would have to keep up the pace to save his skin. It was only when he felt a cold hand touch his shoulder that Beorf transformed into a bear. Breathlessly, he followed the path that led him safely through the deadly weapons. Suspecting nothing, the gorgons ploughed straight into the forest of blades at full speed. It was a massacre that left no survivors.

Satisfied with his work, Beorf headed for home. Planning to spend the rest of the night safe in the library, he opened the trap door and climbed down the ladder. As he felt for his firefly lamp, a red light lit up the room.

Sitting at his father's desk was what looked like a bald man, staring straight at Beorf. His bright eyes were pale yellow, and their elongated pupils constantly dilated and contracted. His hands, arms and neck, even the back of his head, were covered in scales, and his eyebrows met above his nose, just like Beorf's own. He had long, terrible nails, and serpent's teeth, through which his forked tongue flicked. Around his neck were dozens of gold necklaces studded with precious gems, and he wore two large, shiny, golden earrings. Naked from the waist up, he had a muscular torso, but his legless body ended in a very long, grey serpent's tail…

Beorf immediately turned to flee from this monstrous creature, but he was seized by the creature's huge tail, which held him tight.

'Ssss…Leaving already, my young friend?' the serpent-man said, its voice more like a hiss. 'It'sss very rude of you to flee from my presssence before I've even introduced myssself.'

The tail released its grip and Beorf, trembling, turned to face the creature.

'Well, sss, you're a brave boy. That'sss very good. My name is Karmakasss and I have journeyed, sss, a very long way to get here. Don't be afraid, young friend, I mean you, sss, no harm. Look, I'm jussst the sssame as you – what the humansss call a manimal. I would never hurt sssomeone from my own race without a good reason. You seem sssurprised to see me! Is thisss the first time you have seen another member of your own ssspecies?'

Unable to utter a single word, Beorf just nodded his head.

'That'sss very unfortunate. You know why beings like usss are disssappearing one after another? It'sss because they are hunted by humans. Men are jealousss of our giftsss, jealousss of our power. I am a naga, sss, a ssserpent, in the ancient language. You are a beorite, a man-bear. You possess power over beesss, and other insectsss. I have power over everything that crawlsss, that bitesss and that hasss venom. I control the gorgonsss because of their hair. But I will confess a sssecret that perhapsss you already know? I'm alssso a powerful magician. Don't worry, I'm a good wizard. I only hurt people who have, sss, hurt me. I only become unpleasant when sssomeone is unpleasant to me.'

Beorf's hands were clammy and his heart pounded. In a trembling voice, he interrupted the strange wizard.

'So why did your army of gorgons change all the inhabitants of the kingdom into stone statues? Is it just because you wanted to get your pendant back and avenge yourself on Yaune the Purifier? You didn't have to punish so many innocent people to quench your thirst for revenge!'

Karmakas let out a laugh that chilled Beorf to the bone.

'Oh, he'sss clever, the little beorite! I think we were wrong, in my country, to consider the bear-men as the most ssstupid members of the manimal race. You're not as ssstupid as you look, my fat bumpkin bear! The inhabitantsss of the kingdom were transformed into ssstatues for trusting a thief and a murderer. Let me tell you my version of the ssstory and you will undersssstand better. I was living peacefully in my village, a village that no longer existsss today. In the heart of a desert of ssstones, the nagas lived in peace with the humans who lived in the sssprawling neighbouring town. We were craftsmen and we had a ssspecial talent for working with gold. We also had minesss and great riches.

'The humans finally became jealousss of our treasures and called on the Knightsss of the Light to exterminate usss and sssteal our wealth. Fortunately, the gorgonsss came to our assistance, but it was too late. My wife and my fifteen children, all nagasss, were killed by the knights. Then we killed the knights, and only Yaune the Purifier managed to sssave his skin. Do you know how? Becaussse, during the final great battle against the gorgonsss, Yaune was in one of our temples, ssstealing our treasures! If he had taken part in the battle, he would have died too, petrified by the gorgonsss. That pendant belongsss to my people and I'm here to retrieve what was ssstolen. That'sss all. The creatures of my race, those that have sssurvived, wanted to take revenge on men and make them pay for their greed, for their inability to accssept those who are different from themssselves. Didn't the Knights of the Light kill your father and mother, too, jussst because they were different from them?'

At these words, Beorf started crying.

'You sssee, we're alike,' the naga continued. 'We are both victimsss of humansss and we have to combine our forcesss against that powerful enemy. Just imagine, the bear and the ssserpent united to avenge the manimals! Come, let me hug you. I'll be your new father. Ssss.'

Regaining his confidence, Beorf looked Karmakas straight in the eye.

'It's true my parents were killed by humans,' he said. 'It's also true that men are sometimes narrow-minded and refuse to accept the things they don't understand. My father told me many stories about manimals but he always told me to be suspicious of the snake-men. He said that it was mainly due to the snake-men's lies and thirst for power that humans began hunting manimals. I had a father and now he's dead. I don't need you to replace him. You're just trying to win my trust so you can get your pendant back. Beorites may not be as intelligent as nagas, but we know the difference between good and evil. I've hidden the pendant and you'll never get your hands on it!'

The magician clenched his teeth, tensed his muscles and reared up on his huge tail.

'I'll find a way to make you talk, sss, you impertinent wretch! You've just sssigned your own death sssentence!'

CHAPTER TEN

THE STORYTELLER

An old man sat on a bench, surrounded by children. He began his story: 'Once upon a time, long, long ago, there was a young man named Junos. He lived with his mother in a little hut in the forest. This boy had no talent at all. He was always getting the wrong end of the stick, and he drove his mother to despair. His father had died many years before, and the poor woman was left to take care of everything, from the cooking and cleaning to the farm chores. She did absolutely everything possible to ensure that she and her good-for-nothing son survived. Junos spent his days hanging about in the fields, smelling the flowers and chasing butterflies.

'Then one day, seeing his mother toiling at her chores, he said:

"Mother, I'm going to town to find work. That way, with the money I earn, you'll finally be able to rest."

"But Junos, you don't know how to do anything with your hands," answered his mother. "And you always manage to mess things up."

"You'll see what I can do, mama," Junos replied.

The storyteller had the full attention of his audience. Amos, who was walking by, stopped to listen.

'So Junos headed for town. He stopped at all the shops, all the farms, and all the craftsmen's workshops. He asked everyone for work, but each time someone asked what he could do, Junos answered honestly: "Nothing." When they heard that, of course, nobody wanted to hire him! At the last farm he went to, Junos thought of his mother, who often scolded him for doing anything at all. So when the farmer asked him what he could do, Junos answered, without lying: "Sir, I do anything at all!" He was hired immediately.'

In the little square, the crowd of curious listeners was getting bigger. Even adults were waiting with interest to hear the rest of the story.

'All that day, Junos and the farmer worked hard chopping wood and hoeing the garden. When evening came, the boy received a shiny coin as his wages. As he walked home, pleased with his first day at work, Junos played with the coin, tossing it into the air and catching it. Then, fumbling a catch, he lost the coin in a stream that ran alongside the road. Junos returned home and sadly told his mother about his misadventure.

"Next time, Junos, take what the farmer gives you and put it in your pocket straight away," she told him.

'Junos promised, and next day he returned to the farm. This time, he milked the cows. In exchange for his labour, the farmer gave him a bucket of fresh milk. Junos did exactly what his mother had told him to do. He put the milk in his pocket so that he wouldn't lose any on his way home! Junos arrived home completely soaked – even his shoes were full of milk. As she listened to her son's story, his poor mother choked back her anger.

"You should always leave whatever the farmer gives you in its container, son. Do you understand?"

'Junos nodded. Next day, when he finished work, he was given a big lump of butter. So that it wouldn't melt in the sun, the farmer asked Junos for his hat and put the butter inside it. The boy put the hat back on his head and ran quickly home. But the heat from his head had melted the butter, and he appeared before his mother dripping with yellow grease!'

A sizeable crowd had now gathered around the old man. Everyone seemed to be enjoying the story about the dim-witted boy. The storyteller was an expert, playing every one of the characters and miming expressions. He certainly knew how to keep his audience's attention.

'When Junos had finished explaining, his mother said

to him: "You were right to leave the butter in your hat, but you shouldn't have put it on your head! Take this big bag. Next time, put whatever you get from the farmer in the bag and carry it on your back. Do you understand, Junos?"

'The boy answered yes, he understood perfectly, and set off. Close to the farm where he worked, there was a magnificent castle. Junos admired it every time he passed by, and sometimes dreamed that one day he'd earn enough money to live there. He'd noticed, too, that there was always a young girl sitting outside on one of the balconies, weeping. Junos wondered why she was so sad but didn't give it too much thought.

'The day came when the farmer didn't need Junos any more. Generously he gave the boy a donkey to thank him for all he had done for him. The boy was thrilled. Remembering that his mother had told him to put whatever the farmer gave him in the bag, he tried to stuff the donkey inside. He tried one hoof first and then the other, but soon realized the bag was much too small to hold a whole donkey. So Junos thought of another solution. He put the bag over the donkey's head, then crouched down and crawled underneath the animal, intending to carry it on his back. He wanted his mother to be proud of him and, for once, he was going to do things the right way. The donkey, with the bag on its head and Junos underneath, brayed and thrashed about. With great difficulty Junos got to his feet, but just as he managed to get the donkey off the ground, they both fell down in a heap.

'As he tried to load the beast onto his back a second time, the boy noticed a man approaching. It was the king who lived in the nearby castle. He greeted Junos politely and introduced himself. Then he told Junos that his daughter had not stopped crying for years. He had promised her hand in marriage to anyone who could make her smile. It seemed that from high on her balcony the princess had seen Junos' antics with the donkey, begun laughing uncontrollably and couldn't stop! And that is how Junos came to marry the princess, become king, and live in the castle with his mother. So, my dear friends, this just goes to show that to become king, all you need is to know how to do nothing – or anything at all!'

To thunderous applause, the storyteller bowed to his audience and walked around holding out his hat to them. He received a few coins, and some of the people coming from the market gave him bread, vegetables and eggs. Someone even gave him a sausage. As Amos turned to leave the square, the storyteller called out to him.

'You listened to my story, young man, and yet you are giving me nothing?'

'I have very little myself, sir,' answered Amos. 'I'm searching for my parents and I've just arrived from a far-away land. Your story certainly deserves more than just my applause, but unfortunately that's all I can give you.'

'I already have everything I need in this hat,' the old man replied pleasantly. 'In fact, all I lack is company. Would you do me the honour of sharing my food with me?'

'Gladly!' answered Amos, who was famished.

'My name is Junos,' said the storyteller. 'And you, young man, what's your name?'

'Is your name really Junos?' Amos asked, surprised to hear that name again. 'Like the character in your story?'

'My friend, I draw my inspiration from wherever I find it. All of my heroes, from the dimmest to the most intelligent, have my name. It reminds me of when my father used to tell me stories. All the heroes in his tales also had my name.'

'My name is Amos Daragon, and I'm delighted to make your acquaintance,' said Amos.

'Likewise,' said the old man. 'You see, my lad, I tell tales to earn my living, it's all I know how to do. And I'm always looking for good stories. Tell me where you've come from and what you're doing here. And tell me how you lost your parents. I'm interested because I lost mine, too, a few years ago.'

Amos felt at once that he could trust Junos. The old man's sparkling eyes had a youthful look about them.

Apart from the old lady in white he'd met at the neighbouring village fountain, it had been several days since Amos had spoken to anyone, and he was happy to meet this friendly chap. Before he began his story, Amos warned the old man that he might not believe everything he was going to hear, but swore that it was nothing but the truth. As he tucked into the food the old man offered him, Amos told him about the Kingdom of Omain, about his conversation with the mermaid in the Bay of Caves, and about the mission she had given him. He also told him how he had fooled Lord Edonf, and about his escapades in Great Bratel and with Barthelemy, who was now, like all the others, a stone statue.

Then he talked about meeting Beorf, about Yaune the Purifier's Game of Truth, the blind cat, the druid with the mushroom growing from his neck, the gorgons, and the book he had found in the secret library of Beorf's father. He recounted the story of the pendant and how he had entrusted it to Beorf so it would not fall into the hands of the gorgons, and then he told of his departure from Great Bratel. He could not hide his regret at having to leave his friend behind in the city of statues. Amos also revealed what he had learned about the basilisk.

He told Junos everything, right down to the smallest detail. But it all seemed so long ago! He felt as though he was telling a story from years past – his experiences seemed so very far off. The sun was setting by the time

Amos ended his tale. It had been a good three hours since he and Junos had begun their conversation. Intrigued by the boy's story, the old man had asked many questions.

'That was an excellent story,' said the storyteller when he was finally satisfied. 'And to tell you the truth, I believed every word of it. Now I'll tell you one about Tarkasis Forest, and I hope you'll believe me too. I stopped telling this story many years ago because nobody believed it – people thought I was crazy. So I decided to keep the truth to myself and just tell made-up tales in future. Would you like to hear a true story of great misfortune?'

Amos, his stomach full and thrilled to have such an interesting person to talk to, was overjoyed.

'I'm listening, and I can assure you I'm ready to believe everything you tell me.'

'Very long ago,' began the old man, 'very close to Tarkasis Forest, there lived a little boy. He had beautiful curly black hair, a big happy smile, a fertile imagination, and a wonderful dog. He loved his dog more than anything in the world. His father farmed the land, and his mother made the best pancakes in the kingdom. The boy's parents were always warning him not to venture into the woods. Evil forces lived there, they said, and anyone who dared to wander in among the trees disappeared! One day the boy heard his dog barking in the woods. Sensing that his pet was in danger, he dashed into the forest without even thinking about his parents' warning. He walked for a very long time. The trees were strangely shaped and there were flowers everywhere. It was the most magnificent forest the boy had ever seen.

'Suddenly, a speck of light sprang out of a flower and began circling the boy. It was only many, many years later that the boy understood that on that day he had entered the kingdom of the fairies. Other lights joined the first one, and as they circled round him, he began to hear wonderful music. A prisoner in the fairy ring, the boy danced with the lights until finally he collapsed from exhaustion and fell asleep under a tree. When he woke up, his hair was white and he had a long beard. He had aged fifty years! He returned home to find that his house had disappeared. He found no trace of his parents, his dog or his thatched cottage. A road now ran through what had been his father's garden. He walked down the road and found himself in a city called Berrion – the city we're in now.

'Completely bewildered, the boy told his story to all passers-by, proclaiming loudly that his youth had been stolen. But no one would listen to him, and for a long time people thought he was crazy. Eventually, he had to accept reluctantly that he was now an old man and he began telling stories in order to survive. That little boy is still alive today and, like all the heroes in all my stories, his name is Junos. In fact, you're talking to him right now! That was my own story I told you. Will you be the first person to believe my adventure?'

Amos was amazed to realize he had already heard this story. His father had told it to him when they left the Kingdom of Omain. Urban Daragon had met this old storyteller years before while he was travelling with Frilla.

'I believe your story and I promise here and now to give you back the youth you have been seeking for so long,' said Amos, and he saw two streams of tears running down the old man's cheeks. 'Take me to Tarkasis Forest and I will right the wrong that you have suffered.'

CHAPTER ELEVEN

TARKASIS FOREST

J unos invited Amos to spend the night with him in the little room he had rented at a run-down inn in Berrion. The old man apologized to his guest for the lack of comfort. Before they fell asleep, they talked together for a long time, mostly about fairies. Junos knew many stories and legends about the fairies.

According to these tales, much of the Earth was ruled in the beginning by races of ogres, goblins and trolls called fomorians and firbolgs. Then, for reasons long forgotten, the fairies arrived from the West, probably carried by the wind from the oceans. They fought the goblins and the trolls, and finally succeeded in weakening the ogres enough to force them into exile. The ogres migrated to the North, to the cold lands of the barbarians.

Then the humans came from the East. They were powerful warriors who rode magnificent horses. They took over the farmland and forced the fairies to take refuge in the forests. A few fairies made friends with the humans, but most remained in the forests, where they lived in seclusion and kept clear of humans. Their kingdoms were secret and hard to find. Like bees, fairies observed a strict social hierarchy with a queen, workers and warriors.

There were men, however, who worked in harmony with the forest creatures. These men were called druids. Their task was to protect nature, the forests and its creatures, including the various fairy kingdoms. The fairies chose certain humans to become druids. They stole babies from their cradles, replacing them with enchanted wooden dolls which looked like real infants, so that parents believed that their babies were sleeping safely in their beds. These substitute children appeared quite normal until one day they just died for no apparent reason. Even today, there's one particular custom that the inhabitants of Berrion still observe. Although few of them really believe in supernatural beings, parents still hang open scissors over their children's beds to protect them. The blades cut down any fairies that try to fly near the cradle. They also tie bells, red ribbons and garish garlands onto their babies' clothing. The tinkling of the bells will immediately warn the parents if fairies try to kidnap a baby, and it's thought that the bright ribbons and garlands prevent fairies from flying straight.

Amos then asked Junos if he knew anything about the mask wearers. Junos replied that he had once heard of a man who vanquished a dragon single-handedly. They had called the man 'the Wearer', but the legend did not tell anything more.

Exhausted, Amos finally fell asleep on the old straw mattress Junos had laid on the floor. He dreamed about the woman who had given him buns and eggs at the fountain. In the dream, she was still wearing her white dress but now she was young. She kept repeating the same phrase: 'Drive the trident into the stone and open the passageway. Drive the trident into the stone and open the passageway!'

Who was the woman in white, and why she was speaking to him? What was all this about the stone and the passageway? Amos longed to decipher the meaning of this phrase she kept repeating, but he stood speechless, unable to utter a single word, and the woman in white disappeared. Amos woke and for the rest of the night he lay pondering on his dream. When Junos awoke, the two companions ate breakfast, then set out for Tarkasis Forest.

After walking for a few hours, Amos and Junos arrived at the edge of a forest.

'This is it,' declared the old man. 'This is where I used to live. It looks very different now, but some things haven't changed – those big boulders are the same, and that oak tree was already well grown before I danced with the fairies. I haven't been back here for years, not since I emerged from these woods with the body of an old man. I was just eleven years old...'

These memories made the old man sad, but Amos was still wrapped up in his dream from the night before. It had been too real for an ordinary dream. 'Drive the trident into the stone and open the passageway!' Amos peered at the ground, looking for clues. He examined the trees, noting the different species, and looked closely at the stones.

Then, after several long minutes of silence, he said: 'Junos, it looks as though there's a path here. If you block out the small trees, ferns and other little plants, you can just see it.'

Doing as Amos said, Junos found he could indeed see something that looked like a path, or at least tracks through the undergrowth:

'Yes, I think you're right! Let's follow it.'

They followed the trail until they found their path blocked by enormous pine trees and mighty oaks. No clue as to which way they should go. But then, in the long grass, they saw a large boulder. Coming closer, they saw that in the stone there was a round hole and, slightly above this, three more holes set close together. There was also a narrow slot, and what looked like a large honeycomb cell.

The words of the lady in white came back to Amos from his dream! He took his trident and, with one swift movement, thrust it into the second set of marks. How strange! The three teeth of the ivory trident fitted so perfectly into the row of holes that they might have been made for this purpose.

'And the other holes must be for other weapons, each representing one of the elements,' thought Amos. 'If the first hole represents air, an arrow must fit in there. My trident, the weapon of the mermaid, represents water. The third one is made for a sword, which is forged in fire, and the honeycomb cell must be there for a weapon representing the earth – the shaft of a war mace, I'll bet. Of course! The holes are locks, and the weapons are keys. Four locks, four keys, four ways to open the same door! That's why Crivannia told me to take the trident with me.'

But at that very moment, as the trident drove into the stone, the dense, dark forest around them seemed to tear itself apart. There was a deafening sound of branches cracking and trunks twisting, and Amos and Junos watched in amazement as a long, dark tunnel opened up before them. Amos pulled his weapon from the stone. The door to the heart of Tarkasis Forest was now open, and without a word, the two companions entered the tunnel. After just a few minutes they emerged in a clearing. Flowers bloomed everywhere: on the ground, on the rocks, and among the trees. Fairies of all colours and sizes flew about in all directions, busy with their tasks. The sun's rays were blinding, and a clear, pure light flooded the clearing. Out of the brightness a man appeared, walking slowly towards them. Amos recognized him as the druid he had met in Great Bratel. He was still just as dirty and ugly. With the blind cat on his shoulder, he greeted them with open arms.

'Welcome to the kingdom of Gwenfadrilla, Master Daragon. I see you have brought a friend. I was half expecting you to be accompanied by the young manimal. But let's hurry – the grand council of fairies is now in session. The ladies have been expecting you for some time and they are anxious to meet you. If he wishes, Mr. Junos can come with us. I believe he has already met the fairies!' he added, laughing heartily.

The druid led Amos and Junos to the centre of the forest. Inside a circle of seven dolmens, a throng of fairies and druids from far and wide sat comfortably on oversized, strangely shaped wooden chairs. They all applauded Amos' arrival. There were fairies large and small, very old and hairy druids, beautiful young druidesses, young apprentices and strange little creatures covered in wrinkles.

Amos and Junos were invited to sit in the centre of the circle. Before them were two women wearing crowns: a sinewy mermaid with light blue hair, and a tall, slender fairy with pointed ears. Both radiated beauty and an astonishing power and charisma. The fairy with the pointed ears, dressed all in green, stood up and called for silence with a wave of her hand.

'Dear friends. Gwenfadrilla, Queen of Tarkasis Forest, is pleased to welcome you all to her kingdom to witness the revival of the cult of the mask wearers.'

Amos realized that, in the manner of all queens, Gwenfadrilla was talking about herself in the third person.

'The mask wearer was chosen by Crivannia, Princess of the Waters, to accomplish a mission. He was recognized as the chosen one in Great Bratel by our most ancient druid, Mastagan the Muddy, and by the Lady in White. Amos Daragon, who is here today, will become the first mask wearer in a new generation of heroes, charged with restoring balance in this world. Anyone who opposes his appointment must speak now or forever hold their peace!'

The assembly remained silent.

'I oppose this choice!' Amos declared, getting to his feet.

A murmur of astonishment ran through the gathering.

'I refuse to serve anyone without understanding what is expected of me,' Amos went on. 'I don't doubt that you are doing me a great honour, but I must know more about this mission you are entrusting to me. And I need you to explain what a mask wearer is.'

Perplexed, Gwenfadrilla looked at Mastagan the Muddy.

'Mastagan, didn't you tell him anything?'

'Well, yes...a little,' mumbled the druid, 'but not everything. I thought you were supposed to tell him. So, er, I didn't really...'

'Do you mean to tell me the boy has come all this way without knowing what a mask wearer is?' interrupted the queen.

'I think...well, I suppose so!' mumbled the druid, looking at his feet.

Taking advantage of the confusion, Amos took the white stone from his pocket and spoke again.

'First of all, I have come all this way to deliver a message to you. Your friend Crivannia, Princess of the Waters, is dead. Her kingdom has fallen into the hands of the merrows. Before she died, she asked me to give you this white stone and tell you that she has chosen me as mask wearer. But I think you already knew that, didn't you?'

'Yes, I knew that already,' admitted the green fairy. 'Give me the stone and listen to what I have to say. In ancient times, the world was divided between the sun and the moon, between the creatures of the day and the creatures of the night. The beings of the day represented good, and those of the night represented evil.

For centuries, creatures from both sides fought deadly battles for domination over the earth, by day or night. Eventually, weary of this fruitless, endless combat, great kings and queens from the two camps met to work out a solution. In order to re-establish the peace everyone longed for, there had to be a compromise. Together, they selected humans – the only beings in which good and evil co-existed – and created the sacred order of mask wearers.

'Their task, simple enough, it seemed, was to work with good and evil, with day and night, in order to re-establish balance in the world. The warriors of balance undertook missions to slay threatening dragons, calm the passions of unicorns, and reunite kingdoms divided by war. These men drew their powers from the magic of the elements. They each possessed four masks: of air, fire, earth and water. On each of these four masks, four stones of power could be set. Four white stones for the air, four blue ones for water, four red ones for fire and four black ones for earth. In all, sixteen stones of power. The warriors fulfilled their missions well, and for many years good and evil lived in perfect balance. Believing eternal peace had been achieved, we decided there was no further need for more mask wearers. Their masks were abandoned, and the stones of power were shared between the forces of night and the forces of day. Recently, however, the creatures of the night have taken up the battle again. The attack by the merrows against the mermaids is the best example. This is why we have decided to revive the order of the mask wearers.'

Amos stood silent for a moment.

'You spoke earlier of the Lady in White,' he said. 'I saw her twice. Who exactly is she?'

'She is a powerful spirit,' explained Gwenfadrilla. 'She is the conscience that accompanies and guides the warriors of balance. Each mask wearer is a god-child of the Lady in White. She will always be there to protect you and show you which path to follow. Today, if you accept the destiny we have planned for you, I will present you with your first mask, the mask of air. In it you will set the white stone you brought me, and the powers of the ancient object will be revived. Then you must find the other three masks and the fifteen missing stones. The more masks and stones you have, the greater will be your power and the better you will control the elements. Amos Daragon, do you accept our proposal?'

There was total silence as Amos considered her words. The fairies held their breath and stood still. The druids stamped their feet with impatience and the mermaid with the blue hair, the new Princess of the Waters, wondered if Crivannia had done right in choosing this boy.

'I accept – on one condition!' Amos said, on his feet again.

'That is unusual,' Gwenfadrilla replied, 'but we are listening.'

'I want the fairies to return to my friend Junos the youth they stole from him. He must be returned to his family to help his father in his garden and to eat the best pancakes in the world – his mother's. And I want him to find his dog!'

The queen of the fairies smiled.

'Your request is granted. My loyal fairies, return Junos to his home in the past, and make sure he is exactly the same age as when he had the misfortune to fall into our trap.'

Junos leaped for joy and cried like a baby.

'Amos Daragon has given me back my youth! I will have my childhood after all! I'll see my dog again! And my father and mother! Thank you! Oh, thank you, my friend! Thank you with all my heart!'

As he left the council surrounded by a ring of fairies, the old man turned to Amos, his eyes full of tears.

'I will pay you back a hundredfold for what you have done for me,' he said. 'I swear this on my life, on my soul, and on the heads of my parents. Farewell for now, my friend!'

After Junos had gone, Gwenfadrilla solemnly picked up a magnificent crystal mask. It bore the face of a fine-featured man with a high forehead. She handed it to Amos to try on. The mask fitted the boy's face perfectly.

Then she inserted into the mask the white stone of power sent by Crivannia. Amos had the strangest sensation of breathing the rhythm of the wind.

'This mask will grow with you,' declared the queen. 'It is your possession and your most precious asset. It does not yet have its full powers, but you will discover them. When all four stones are set in it, you will have the power to summon hurricanes and to walk on air. Now let us all pay homage to Amos Daragon! Let us feast in honour of the first human in the second generation of the warriors of balance!'

Everyone stood up and applauded as festive music began to play.

CHAPTER TWELVE

BEORF AND MEDUSA

Karmakas had taken up residence in the castle of Great Bratel. With the help of the gorgons, he had moved all its inhabitants, more than a thousand statues, outside the city. They stood on either side of the road leading to the city gates and made a terrifying sight. Peddlers, travellers, adventurers and troubadours refused to venture near the city. All who saw this dreadful spectacle turned back, vowing never again to set foot in that part of the world.

The gorgons had ransacked the city. All the houses had been demolished or burned down. The silence of death now replaced the joyful shouts of children from happier days. There was no life, there were no flowers. All human activity had ceased. Yaune the Purifier's army, the Knights of the Light, had been vanquished forever. A black flag showing a serpent, mouth open and ready to bite, flew above the city. Even the river water had been poisoned; the fields lay fallow, and all the birds had deserted the region.

With his powerful magic Karmakas had doubled his army of gorgons. The city was now teeming with snakes. Cockroaches, the reptiles' favourite food, crawled over the walls of the castle, through the remains of the demolished houses, and all over the battlements of Great Bratel.

Beorf lay buried up to his neck in the market square. His head was the only part of his body that was above ground. He had been blindfolded so that the gaze of the gorgons would not petrify him. For three days he had suffered terrible agonies. At night, monsters trampled on his head to keep him from sleeping, and during the day his skull baked in the blazing sun. Every morning, the nagas came to visit him. Karmakas knew the beorites' only weakness. He knew that the bear-men's great physical resistance and strength could withstand almost anything – except hunger. Every morning, the magician tempted Beorf with bread and honey.

'If you tell me where the pendant isss, I'll give you all the food you want. Tell me where the pendant isss and we will work together. I know you are ssso hungry. Talk to me. Tell me where you have hidden my mossst preciousss possession.'

Although the fat boy's eyes were blindfolded, he could smell the aroma of the fresh bread and imagine the taste of honey on his tongue. His stomach was rumbling with hunger and his whole body cried out for food. His taste buds were stimulated and thick saliva filled his mouth. Every morning his willpower grew weaker in the face of this torture. But day after day Beorf gave the same answer:

'I'll never tell you! I'll sell my soul before you'll get the tiniest bit of information out of me.'

Furious, the nagas would leave the square, hissing with rage.

Towards the end of the fifth day, exhausted by the aching in his stomach and doubting that he could last out another day, Beorf heard a voice in his ear. It was the voice of a young girl.

'Don't be afraid,' she whispered. 'I'm here to help you.'

Beorf felt hands digging to remove the earth around him. The girl was freeing him from his prison.

'First, I must warn you. I'm a gorgon,' she said, helping him climb out of the pit. 'Be careful. Don't try to look into my eyes or you'll be turned to stone. For your safety, I'm wearing a cape with a hood that covers my eyes. I'm going to take your blindfold off now.'

Opening his eyes, Beorf was astonished to see standing before him a young gorgon of great beauty. Even though her hood was pulled down to her nose he could see her pretty face and lovely mouth. Her lips were dark and full. A few pretty snake-heads, golden and showing no malice, poked out from under her hood, making the cloth ripple. Her skin was a pretty pale green.

'Come on, we must get away from this place before the wizard catches us,' she said, holding out her hand to him. 'Do you know how to get out of the city without going through the big gate?'

'Yes, I know a way,' said Beorf. 'Follow me!'

Together they made their way through the tunnel Beorf had dug under the city wall. They ran quickly and reached the forest without any trouble. The fat boy led the young gorgon to a grotto his parents had used as a larder. There, the manimal plunged headfirst into the food, stuffing himself with dried fruit, nuts, honey, grains and salted meat. Only when he was completely full did Beorf remember to offer his rescuer something to eat.

'Thank you,' said the girl. 'But I don't really eat this kind of food. I only eat insects. Cockroaches boiled in toad's blood are my favourite – they're delicious! You obviously like your food. You should try my recipe one day.'

Beorf felt sick at the very thought, but didn't let it show. The colour had returned to his face, and he was now in fine form. His whole body relaxed and he was unable to hold back a resounding belch. The young gorgon laughed a clear, ringing laugh. How could such a charming creature have come from such a horrible race?, thought Beorf. Embarrassed, he apologized.

'Who are you and why did you help me?' he asked.

'You'd never be able to pronounce my real name,' answered the gorgon. 'Call me Medusa. That's what the humans often call the people of my race. It's a name inherited from Princess Medusa, who was transformed into an ugly immortal by an evil goddess. There are many legends, but no one really knows the origins of my species. Your name is Beorf, I know. They say you can transform into a bear. Is that true?'

Flattered that this beautiful young gorgon knew his name, Beorf showed her by transforming at once.

'There!' he said, proud and hairy from head to foot.

'Cover your eyes,' said Medusa. 'I'd like to have a look at you.'

The bear put a paw over his snout, and the young girl took a long look at him.

'Bears are wonderful! I've never seen such animals!' she exclaimed, pulling her hood back down over her eyes. 'Where I come from, there are only gorgons and snakes. And a lot of stone statues,' she added, with her enchanting laugh. 'But to answer your question, I helped you because I also need help. Karmakas is an evil wizard and he uses his magic to keep total control over my people. He forced us to come to this kingdom to carry out his wishes. If we defy his orders, he forces the snakes in our hair to bite our shoulders and necks. It hurts so much that our screams even make the mountains shake.

'We might be creatures of the night who can't stand the sun, but that doesn't mean we're evil and cruel. We know we have the power to turn living creatures to stone, so to prevent such misfortunes happening, my people live hidden in the arid hills and deserts in the East. It was the gorgons themselves who sent me to free you. Please believe me. We don't mean any harm to anyone. And we know how to bring the statues back to life. It's difficult, but it can be done. We don't want to fight any more. We just want to go home and live in peace. But we can't fight Karmakas. Our power doesn't work on him; we are his prisoners, his slaves. We must obey him or endure terrible suffering. Look at my skin and you'll see what I mean.'

Medusa pulled open the collar of her dress. Her neck and shoulders were covered with gaping wounds and scars.

'You see?' she said. 'It's hard for me to believe it's my own hair that does that to me. And yet I love it so much!'

'Why don't you cut the horrible creatures off?' Beorf asked naively, back in his human form.

'Would you cut off an arm or a leg if it caused you pain?' she answered, a little angry. 'My hair is part of me, and every one of the golden snakes you see represents part of my being. Cutting them off would mean certain death. They are my only friends and my sole comfort. I have known them since I was very little and each one has a name. I feed them and care for them.'

'Then can I ask you something?' said Beorf, politely.

'Whatever you want,' replied Medusa.

'I would love to see your eyes, your face.'

The gorgon laughed her pretty laugh again.

'But don't you listen to what you're told, young bear? It's impossible, you'd be turned to stone in a second!'

'I know you can look at a gorgon in a mirror,' Beorf said, proudly. 'I know it because I've done it before by accident. I've got a mirror here and...'

At this, Medusa was panic-stricken.

'You've got a mirror! You've got a mirror! Did you bring me here to kill me? I knew I shouldn't have trusted you! I told the gorgons they must always be suspicious of anything resembling a human. You're evil – you always want to kill any creature different from yourself! If you want to murder me, do it now, but stop torturing me with all this talk of mirrors!'

Beorf had noticed the mirror only a moment earlier, lying among the remains of the food. Now he rushed over, grabbed it and smashed it to the floor. He jumped on it with both feet, shattering it into a thousand pieces.

'There! The mirror's gone! You're safe! There's no more danger! Just calm down – please! I didn't mean to offend or threaten you. I only thought of the mirror because I think you're very beautiful and I wanted to see your eyes. That's all, I swear!'

Medusa grew calmer, but beads of sweat were running down her neck.

'Remember, Beorf, always remember that people of my race are scared to death of mirrors,' said the gorgon, weighing her words carefully. 'A gorgon must never see her own reflection in a mirror, or she will die immediately. We are torn apart from the inside out and crumble into dust. It's the worst death you could possibly imagine. I'd rather cut the snakes from my head one by one than know I'm in a place where there's a mirror.'

'That's okay, I've never liked girls who spend all their time looking in the mirror!' laughed the fat boy, awkwardly. 'But tell me, Medusa,' he went on after a few seconds of embarrassed silence. 'There's something I don't understand. I've already seen gorgons in the forest and...er...how can I put this? Well, they were...shall we say...not exactly pleasant to look at, while you...'

The young gorgon started laughing again.

'I see what you're getting at. Well, at the age of nineteen-and-a-half, the exact age when Medusa was struck by Ceto's curse, our faces change. We become just as ugly as Medusa did then. No one knows why it happens, but very few of us escape the evil spell.'

'Maybe you'll discover it before you reach that age.'

Medusa looked pensive for a moment.

'You're nice, Beorf, did you know that?' she said affectionately.

Beorf grinned broadly.

'Yes, I know.' he answered, blushing.

CHAPTER THIRTEEN

RETURN TO BERRION

During the fairy celebrations that followed the ceremony, Amos found himself eating food he had never tasted before in his life. And for the first time, he drank the nectar of daffodils, daisies and lilies. There was also a concert performed in his honour. The fairy music was sublime, it was so pure and refined, with strange melodies. 'It's hardly surprising that Junos was bewitched,' he thought, recalling his friend's adventure in the woods. Amos fell asleep on the grass to the sound of the celestial music.

The next morning, the fairies brought him a tall glass of dew and a piece of rose-petal cake. Amos set out from the fairy kingdom with his mask, set with its first white stone, and his ivory trident. He made his way back through the long tunnel that had led him into Tarkasis Forest. When he reached the edge of the forest he was surprised to see signs saying: 'No admittance to the forest by royal decree.' Bewildered, he went back along the road – it was now paved.

'This can't have happened overnight!' he said to himself. He was even more surprised, however, when he reached the outskirts of Berrion. The hamlet was now three times the size it had been, and stately walls had been erected around it. Over the roof of a recently constructed castle flew a standard featuring a moon and a sun within a circle. At the city gate, Amos was stopped by a guard.

'By royal decree, all children who wish to enter within the walls of this city must state their name.'

Amos couldn't believe his eyes or his ears. The last time he'd been here, Berrion had had no army, much less these powerful knights wearing magnificent armour and wielding long lances! How could things have changed so much in just one night? Amos remembered that Junos, bewitched by the fairies' spell, had danced for almost fifty years in Tarkasis Forest and emerged an old man. Amos, however, was still a child. He was certain he had not fallen under the same spell as Junos. It was the world around him that had changed.

'My name is Amos Daragon,' he said shyly.

'Repeat your name, young man, if you please!' the guard demanded.

'Ahh... Amos, Amos Daragon.'

'If that is truly your name, you must follow me immediately.'

Without resisting, Amos accompanied the guard into the city and up to the castle. Everything had changed. Houses, inns, shops, marketplace, streets, people – all were completely different. The day before, he had left a large village where people were barely able to eke out a living. Today he found himself strolling through the streets of a fortified city where everyone seemed to be prospering. He just couldn't understand it.

When they reached the castle, the guard led him into a huge hall with a throne at one end. Amos was still looking around in confusion when suddenly the great hall doors were flung open. A middle-aged man ran over to Amos, grabbed him and lifted him high in the air, shouting with joy.

'Amos! My friend! You're back! How are you? I've been waiting for you for so long! This is a great day! What a joy it is to see you again!'

When he finally put Amos down, the boy was amazed to see that it was Junos who stood before him. But he was ten years younger, far sturdier, and his face was beaming with joy.

'But, Junos,' said Amos, 'could you please explain what on earth's going on? Yesterday you recovered your youth – and now you're older again. Did you find your parents and your dog? What happened? You were a storyteller and now you're a king? I don't understand any of this, Junos!'

Junos smiled at his young friend's questions.

'Sit down in my chair while I explain it to you.'

Amos sat on the throne.

'If you became king, Junos, it's because you know how to do nothing or because you got into the habit of doing just anything!'

The hall echoed with Junos' laughter.

'My story! You remembered my story? That was a good one! It's been years since I've told it. I'm not sure if I even remember it myself!'

'For goodness' sake tell me what's going on, Junos, and after that I'll refresh your memory. You told me that story yourself just two days ago, when you looked like an old man. Now you look to be in the prime of life.'

'If you like,' said Junos, taking a deep breath, 'I'll tell it as I used to, back when I told stories for a living. I was older and uglier then than I am today. Alright, here goes!

'Once upon a time there was a young lad who ventured into Tarkasis Forest looking for his dog. He danced with the fairies and became old overnight. He spent twelve years telling stories for a living, and one day he met Amos Daragon, who became his friend. Thanks to Amos, he found his youth again. Up to that point, it's an old story. You know the beginning, but not the end. What comes next is the best part.

'So the boy who'd had almost fifty years of his life stolen became young again. He leaped back five decades! He was returned to the woods exactly one hour after his first encounter with the fairies. He found his dog and his parents again. No one knew he had lived for so many years in the body of a miserable old man. But although he had his child's body back, he kept his adult memory. And since Junos owed so much to his best friend – who, in fact, had not even been born yet! – he vowed to become a knight, and travelled to a neighbouring kingdom to learn the art of combat.

'After many years of loyal service, the noble king asked Junos, who by then had become his foremost knight, what he wanted most in the world. The boy, now a grown man, asked for the lands of Berrion, and requested that a great city be built there. He organised an army, created the Knights of Balance, in wait for you to emerge from the woods so he could finally welcome you. He also had signs put up near Tarkasis Forest so that the fairies would be left in peace.'

'That's marvellous!' exclaimed Amos. 'So you've been waiting for fifty years for me to walk out of this forest?'

'Yes, Amos, I've been waiting for you for fifty years,' the lord and master of Berrion replied. 'You gave me back my youth! Thanks to you, I had a happy childhood and my parents died in my arms, proud of what I had become. Thanks to you, I found my dog again and I loved him and spoiled him for the rest of his life. Thanks to you, I even had time to learn to cook. With my mother's recipe, it's now me who makes the best pancakes in the kingdom! I still remember the great council of the fairies I attended. I know your mission and the task that awaits you. I also remember what you said to me, so long ago, about Great Bratel falling into the hands of the gorgons. I sent my men to confirm it, and then I created the Order of the Knights of Balance to serve you and help you with your mission. An army of four hundred men awaits your orders, my dear mask wearer!'

Amos could hardly believe his ears. Everything was happening so fast.

'Ah yes,' continued Junos, a mischievous glint in his eye. 'I also asked my men to comb all the lands of Berrion, and we, er…found your parents. They're in one of these chambers somewhere. Would you like to go and see them?'

The reunion was charged with emotion. Amos threw himself into the arms of his parents and for a long time they just hugged each other and danced with joy. Then Urban explained to his son how he and his wife had fled Great Bratel just in time. They packed their bags and loaded them onto a horse. Then, knowing where Barthelemy's armour was stored, Urban stole one of the suits. He presented himself at the city gate as a knight, sitting proudly on his steed. Frilla walked beside the horse with her hands tied behind her back, pretending to be his prisoner. Urban ordered that the gates of the city be opened so that he could drive out the mother of the two children who had been expelled earlier. Asking no questions, the guard opened the gates. As soon as they were through, Frilla untied her fake bonds and jumped onto the horse, and the couple fled into the night. The guard, who had been so easily fooled, never reported the incident. And that was how Urban and Frilla managed to get away before the attack of the gorgons.

Amos wanted to tell his own story but Junos had taken care of that. Urban and Frilla already knew the details of their meeting and their journey to Tarkasis Forest.

That evening, before settling down to sleep in the huge bedchamber Junos had reserved for him, Amos put on his mask once again. As he was alone, it seemed like a good time to try it out. He hadn't noticed before that the mask disappeared completely when it came in contact with his skin. Looking at himself now in the mirror, Amos was astonished to see that even though he could feel the mask on his face, it was invisible to the human eye. Just to confirm this, he opened the door of his room and called on a guard to help him open a jammed window. The man came and did so, apparently without noticing anything unusual about Amos' appearance.

When the guard had gone, Amos felt dizzy. His breathing wasn't the same as usual. It felt as though air was entering his body through all his pores. When he looked up, he saw the Lady in White – now only eight years old and playing with the pillows on the bed.

'Don't worry, the mask will adjust to you,' she said nonchalantly. 'It will take a while for it to get used to you. Right now it's probing you and soon it will make contact with your mind. When it does, look out – it's a shock!'

She had hardly uttered these words when pain shot through Amos like a bolt of lightning. It was so intense that he cried out and fell to his knees, paralysed by an ache that seemed to get stronger and stronger. It was torture! After what seemed like an eternity, but was really only moments, the pain subsided and Amos was able to stagger to his feet. The little girl in white was now jumping up and down on the bed.

'It's over!' she said. 'You'll never be able to take that mask off your face again. The other masks, if you find them, fit over that one. You have the power of the wind in you now! That force will return to the mask only with your death. Now come with me!'

Taking Amos by the hand, she led him to the balcony that led off the room. From there they had a magnificent view of the city of Berrion. It was dark now, and torches and bonfires illuminated the city's night-time activities.

'Go on,' she said. 'Try raising the wind!'

Amos held out his left arm. A strong, steady breeze made the torch flames flicker throughout the city.

'Well,' said the Girl in White, 'you seem to have got the hang of it. I don't think you need me any more. You'll find that you can also blow quite hard from your mouth. That's good for propelling your trident, or any other weapon, a great distance. And when you speak, your words can travel many miles. The birds are now your friends, but you must not take advantage of their trust!'

With this, the Girl in White ran to the bed, flung back the blankets and disappeared under the sheets. Yet again, Amos had failed to get a word in edgeways.

Amos opened his eyes and sat bolt upright. He was in his bed and it was morning. He could no longer feel the mask on his face. He looked around him. The mask had gone. Looking in the mirror, he saw nothing but the reflection of his bare face. A bluetit was sunbathing on the balcony, and Amos walked over to it. The bird did not seem in the least bit afraid. Amos held out his hand and asked it softly, in a low, gentle voice, if it would come to him. At once, the little bird fluttered off the railing to perch on his hand.

'So,' he thought. 'Everything I experienced last night was real! It wasn't a dream. The mask has blended with my body and I now possess all its powers. And to think that, at the moment, the mask only has one of its four stones! It's hard to imagine what my power will be when I have the other three. Not to mention the other three masks, of earth, fire and water. I only hope I live long enough to find them all and accomplish what's expected of me!'

He saw a crow flying by. It nodded a greeting to Amos and continued on its way. Leaning over the balcony railing, he saw that in a little square nearby, a dozen or so children were trying in vain to fly a kite. Amos raised his left hand and concentrated. As the wind carried the kite high into the air, the children shouted with joy. After a few minutes, though, the young mask wearer lost his concentration and the kite fell straight down onto the nose of a passer-by. Dizzy, Amos slumped to the floor and the bluetit flew away.

'The magic of the elements is certainly tiring,' he thought. 'It takes such concentration to maintain a spell for very long. If what happened last night wasn't a dream, there's one other thing I must try this morning.'

Amos gathered air into his hands, just as if he was making a snowball. He placed the transparent sphere in his mouth and trapped a message inside.

'Beorf,' he whispered, 'it's me, Amos. I'm fine, and I'll come to you as fast as I can. I've got an army of four hundred men! Hang on, my friend – I'll soon be with you.'

When he had finished his message, Amos could see the words whirling around inside the ball. Then he threw it with all his might.

'Go to the ear of my friend Beorf!' he said.

Amos watched the ball fly towards Great Bratel. He hoped with all his heart that his friend was still alive. He missed Beorf terribly, and he bitterly regretted being separated from him. Lost in thought but suddenly feeling hungry, Amos headed for the dining room. There he found Junos, helping his servants clear the tables after breakfast.

'I've asked my men to be ready to leave at a minute's notice. The road is long and there will be many dangers awaiting us. We'll have to be well rested if we want to reclaim Great Bratel from the forces of evil. We can discuss our strategy later. Long live the Knights of Balance!'

But as Amos looked at Junos, his eyes rolled and he fell unconscious to the floor. His magic tricks had drained him of all his energy.

CHAPTER FOURTEEN

THE EYES OF MEDUSA

or three days, Beorf and Medusa had been sharing the same hiding place, only leaving the grotto once. Violent storms and strong rain kept them confined to their rather uncomfortable abode, but there were enough provisions in the larder for the boy to survive for several weeks, while the young gorgon had to make do with the insects she found in the cave. She wasn't exactly happy with this diet, though, and would have preferred more cockroaches and fewer spiders.

They spent a great deal of time talking. Beorf told his new friend about his life in the forest with his parents, and about his games with the bees. As time passed, Beorf grew to like Medusa more and more. He hadn't had many opportunities to make friends, and her presence filled his heart with great happiness. She was sweet and considerate, calm and good-natured.

Using straw and little pieces of wood, Beorf made a charming doll that looked just like Medusa. She was delighted, and kissed him tenderly on the cheek. Beorf wished they could stay in the grotto together forever. Medusa made him feel respected and wanted, and he realized he was in love with her. Medusa's words were music to his ears. Each night they slept back-to-back for warmth. For the boy, it was a life of endless bliss. Time flew, the hours went by like minutes, and the days raced by like hours.

On the morning of the fourth day, Medusa asked Beorf if he knew why the wizard was so interested in Great Bratel.

'Oh yes, I know!' he answered, stuffing hazelnuts into his mouth. 'He's looking for a pendant. But don't worry, he'll never find it!'

'How d'you know?' asked the gorgon, surprised at his confidence.

'Because I hid it really well!' said Beorf, proudly. 'I don't know what the pendant represents for the serpent-man, or what its powers are. He told me a story about it once, but I didn't believe a word of it. You can never trust a naga. They're cunning and they're liars.'

'But if we had the pendant, we could use it against him!' said Medusa, after a moment of thought. 'I know some magic and if I could see the pendant, maybe it would help us understand its powers.'

'I think it would be more dangerous to have it in our possession than to leave it where it is, well hidden. Karmakas is probably capable of sensing its presence and he'd be after us in no time.'

'Yes, you're right, my friend,' Medusa replied. 'But I'm still curious about where you could have hidden the pendant to stop him finding it.'

'I'd love to tell you, but I'm not going to. If Karmakas ever captured you, he'd torture you to make you talk.'

Annoyed, the young gorgon turned her back on him.

'If he captured me,' she sniffed, 'I'd be killed anyway for helping you escape. I understand you want to keep the hiding place a secret. But I thought I was your friend. Among my people, we tell our friends everything. But maybe you're right not to trust me. I'm just an evil gorgon after all!'

'Of course you're my friend!' Beorf said, bewildered. 'You're my best friend! It's only to protect you that I won't tell you where I hid it.'

'I'm sorry,' Medusa said at last. 'I know you're doing it for my own good. I'm just so curious, and I admire you so much! I'd love to know what trick you found to keep the wizard from finding his pendant. That's all.'

Beorf was touched by the compliment.

'Very well, I'll tell you where it is. It will be our secret. When I hid the pendant, I hadn't yet met Karmakas but my friend Amos told me that someone, or something, very powerful would be looking for it. When I found myself alone after he left for Tarkasis Forest, I thought of a place where no one would ever think of looking. It's in the Great Bratel cemetery! It's a real labyrinth – there are thousands of graves and dozens of vaults. I certainly wasn't short of hiding places. The cemetery is just a ten-minute walk from the city. I thought the gorgons would never think to question the dead, and I was right. I'm sure the wizard will never think of looking there!'

Medusa smiled affectionately.

'Thank you for trusting me, my dear friend. I won't share our secret with anyone else. But just tell me one thing more: where in the cemetery did you hide it?'

'Now that I would rather keep to myself,' answered Beorf. 'It's difficult to explain to someone who doesn't know the place. But I'll show you later, if you like. I used to go there a lot with my bees because the flowers are always full of pollen...'

But before he could finish, there was a crash and Karmakas burst into the cave. His long serpent's tail was gone and he was walking on two legs. With one swift movement he grabbed Medusa and held a dagger to her throat.

'Ssss…About time! I have been watching you for three daysss. My patience hasss run out. Now, young beorite, you're going to go to that sscemetery and bring me back my pendant. Or elssse I'll kill your little friend.

After all, one gorgon more or lessss makes no difference for my army.'

'Don't give in to his blackmail,' Medusa said calmly, ignoring the blade at her throat 'Beorf, don't tell him anything! If you save my life, you will endanger many, many others! Let him kill me. Once he has the pendant, he'll kill us anyway. Save your own life and keep quiet!'

Speechless, Beorf did not know what to do.

'Think fast!' said Karmakas, slowly pressing the blade into Medusa's skin. She howled with pain. Beorf could not stand seeing his friend suffer.

'Alright! Let her live and I'll give you the pendant!' he shouted. 'Swear to me you won't hurt her!'

'I ssswear it,' answered the naga. 'I'll wait here with her, to make sssure you come back. Go and get my pendant and be quick about it. I'm running out of patiencessss!'

Changing into his bear form, Beorf bounded out of the grotto. He ran as fast as he could to Great Bratel cemetery, desperately trying to think of a way to get out of this situation.

'If only Amos were here!' he thought. 'He'd find a way to keep the pendant and save Medusa.' One thing was clear in his mind: the gorgon must not die. He would do everything in his power to keep her alive and close to him. Beorf loved Medusa and was ready to give his own life to save hers.

When he reached the cemetery, Beorf crawled into the burial vault of one of the leading city families. Pulling out a stone whose mortar had crumbled away over the years, he quickly recovered the pendant. With the precious object clasped between his paws, he paused for a moment to catch his breath. His head was spinning, and he was tormented by the fear of losing Medusa. He was cornered! The naga had no reason to let them live once he had recovered his possession. Beorf had done everything he could to keep the wizard from finding the pendant, but now he had no choice. He would face his death with dignity. There was little hope of mercy from Karmakas. With this dark thought, he gripped the pendant between his teeth and headed back.

Once in the grotto, Beorf returned to his human form. Dripping with sweat, he stood before the magician, who was still threatening Medusa with his dagger.

'Here's your pendant!' he said. 'Now spare our lives. If you have to kill someone, take my life in exchange for hers. Just let her live. She has nothing to do with any of this – it's between you and me!'

The magician grabbed the pendant with a monstrous laugh.

'Very well, ssss,' he exclaimed. 'I will take your life and I will let Medusssa live. Does that sssuit you?'

Resigned, Beorf took a deep breath.

'Yes,' he declared solemnly. 'My life for hers!'

The naga appeared to be very amused. He put away his weapon and unveiled Medusa's head.

'You sssee, my beautiful child,' he said, 'how everything hasss worked out perfectly for you!'

The young gorgon hugged the naga and kissed him on the cheek.

'You always told me beorites were stupid and sentimental. Getting him to talk was child's play. I never thought it would be so easy. Thank you for your confidence in me, father, I think I played my role rather well.'

Beorf's jaw dropped. He could not believe either his eyes or his ears. Karmakas looked at the boy with a hideous smile.

'I would like to introduce you to my daughter Medusa. All the gorgonsss are my children. We're just one big happy family!'

Pulling her hood back over her eyes, the young gorgon turned to Beorf.

'Did you really believe you were my friend? I hate all hairy creatures, they disgust me! You stink like a filthy animal and I find you grotesque. I don't love you – I hate you. If you paid attention to your brain rather than your stomach, you'd soon have realized that I was putting on an act. But it was so easy to make you believe I was your friend! I can't take any credit for it, my dear Beorf, you are just stupid!'

'I really loved you, Medusa,' the boy answered,

almost in tears. 'And even though I know you lied to me and I'm going to die, I'll never regret the time I spent with you. They were the most wonderful days of my life.'

'Oh, shut up!' she cried. 'You're pathetic. But I'll give you a present, brave boy. In exchange for the ridiculous doll you made me, I'll grant you one of your wishes. In just a moment, I'll allow you to see my face. My eyes will be the last thing you will ever see before you're turned to stone forever. It would be a pity to deprive you of such a sight!'

With that, Medusa lifted her hood. Beorf did not even consider looking away. He wanted so much to see her eyes. They were blood-red. In the centre of each pupil a light burned like fire. Unable to move, Beorf felt his skin hardening as if ice had flooded through his body.

'You have the most beautiful eyes in the world, Medusa.' Beorf said tenderly, just before he was transformed into a stone statue.

CHAPTER FIFTEEN

THE NEW MISSION

Every day for almost a week, Medusa had visited the grotto where Beorf now stood, petrified and lifeless. She gazed for hours at his innocent face, frozen in stone. Beorf had told her she had the most beautiful eyes in the world, and the gorgon could not get his last words out of her head. He had known her eyes were deadly to him, but Beorf had not flinched. He had given his life out of love for her.

Medusa did not understand his behaviour. Love did not exist among the gorgons. It was a feeling to be avoided – a weakness that other species suffered from. Among her people, love and friendship were ridiculed. Friends were frowned upon, so Medusa had none. The weaker gorgons allied themselves with the stronger ones for survival. In the land of the gorgons, leading the clan and finding food and a safe place to sleep meant that every day was a never-ending power struggle.

Since her earliest childhood, Medusa had known only violence from her own kind. The only creature to give her any kind of affection was her father. Karmakas had gathered the weakest gorgons together and looked after them. In return they served him with complete devotion. He now had a powerful army, in which each member knew her own power and didn't dare defy him. He got all the creatures to call him 'father' and gave ranks to the best fighters. The highest-ranking gorgons were all called 'mother'. By doing this the magician had created a kind of family network that was new to the gorgons.

Beorf had told Medusa a lot about his family, but she still could not understand this kind of relationship. Among her people, there were no males – all the gorgons were women. Legend said that the first gorgon, who had been transformed by Ceto, produced offspring every time a drop of her blood fell to the ground. In fact, gorgons reproduced through their hair. Each hair-serpent on their head was a new gorgon ready to be born. When it reached maturity, the reptile fell to the ground and became, over time, a gorgon. Among Medusa's people, there were no family relationships. Each gorgon stood alone – no question of helping the young ones or looking after the elderly. Life was hard, and only the most vicious, the strongest and the most cunning would survive.

Medusa had not lied to Beorf when she told him Karmakas controlled their hair-snakes with his magic.

If a gorgon disobeyed his orders, the snakes bit her face and shoulders, causing pain so intense that it destroyed the will to rebel or to become independent.

It was Karmakas who had ordered Medusa to free Beorf in the square and convince him that she was his friend. Seeing that the boy still refused to speak in spite of his hunger, the wizard had set this trap for him. Then, through the gorgon's golden hair-snakes, he listened in on all the conversations Medusa and Beorf had had in the grotto. And his trick had worked, because the beorites' hearts were as big as their stomachs!

Now that Karmakas had his pendant, he shut himself up inside the castle of Great Bratel. He ordered that no gorgon should leave the city, but using Beorf's secret passage, Medusa managed to slip out secretly. Every day she went to gaze at the young manimal.

There was something fascinating about the boy. When she looked at Beorf, Medusa felt a strange stirring inside her. It was a feeling of emptiness she had never felt before. Medusa would have liked to hold Beorf in her arms, to watch him as he stuffed himself with hazelnuts. She missed the whirlwind of his words and the warmth of his back against hers. With each visit, this feeling grew stronger and it was becoming increasingly painful. It was not like a serpent bite or a combat wound. It was more intense, and far, far deeper.

She stroked Beorf's stone face for a long time, remembering fondly his wonderful sense of humour and his simplicity. Medusa knew he would never stand beside her alive again. The only way to break the gorgon spell, to return stone to life, was for her to see her own reflection in a mirror and be killed by it. So it was impossible for Medusa to live and see Beorf alive ever again. For the first time in her life, she found herself missing someone. She smiled as she thought about Beorf's buffoonery, and then cried at seeing him trapped like this – the prisoner of her own curse. She felt such guilt at having betrayed her only friend.

One day as Medusa was stroking Beorf's face for the last time before returning to Great Bratel, a gust of wind blew into the grotto. It swirled around the cave, touching every object and brushing the walls. It seemed to be looking for something. The breeze circled around Medusa and then Beorf. It formed a translucent sphere in front of Beorf's head. The message-ball tried to enter Beorf's ear, but it cracked against the hard stone and Medusa heard a boy's voice.

'Beorf, it's me, Amos. I'm fine, and I'll come to you as fast as I can. I've got an army of four hundred men! Hang on, my friend – I'll soon be with you.'

Beorf had told Medusa about his friend Amos, but he'd never mentioned he had such incredible powers. So Amos was bringing an army to reclaim Great Bratel! The young gorgon rushed out of the grotto to warn Karmakas, but halfway to the castle she stopped.

'If I tell the wizard everything,' she thought, 'I'll be betraying Beorf a second time. On the other hand, if I keep quiet, the knights will take the city by surprise, my people will be wiped out, and my own life will be in danger.'

Faced with this dilemma, Medusa sat down to think. She did not want to hurt anyone ever again. Her heart had discovered the power of friendship, only it was too late. Now she held the fate of both humans and gorgons in her hands and she would have to choose sides once and for all. Medusa hurried back to the grotto. Standing in front of Beorf, she gazed at him sadly.

'You also have beautiful eyes, my friend,' she said, with a sigh.

In his new quarters, Karmakas told his gorgon servants that he must not be disturbed for any reason. The naga gazed at his pendant. He caressed it for a long time with his bony fingers, smiling with contentment. At last he had recovered his prized possession. After those long years of searching for Yaune the Purifier, his efforts had been rewarded. His enemies, the Knights of the Light, were now just harmless statues. At last he, Karmakas, would be able to create his basilisk!

He felt a new power inside him, courage mixed with the desire for revenge. He would create a new, living weapon to destroy the humans and establish his reign over the earth. His power would spread from city to city, and from country to country, until he controlled half the world! His armies of gorgons would go north to attack the barbarians, then south to seize the rich, prosperous countries that lay beyond the great sea. Nothing could interfere with his plans now. The gods of darkness would thank him and grant him infinite power. Perhaps he would even be elevated to the rank of demigod of evil!

Karmakas came from a far-off land, near Hyperborea. Humans considered his species of manimal to be demons. He lived in a great city cut from the stone of arid mountains. From a very young age he had shown a special gift for magic and knew better than anyone how to control snakes. Seeing this, his parents enlisted him as a worshipper of the god Seth. He became a powerful wizard, soon outstripping his teachers. Wherever he went, he inspired both awe and terror.

Karmakas was soon proclaimed king and master of the city, and at once he incited the inhabitants to rise up against the humans. His pride and grasping ambition drew him into a ruthless war against all the surrounding kingdoms. Hordes of snake-men sacked towns and villages, leaving behind nothing but misery and desolation. Soon, weary of the endless warfare, some of the manimals of his own species decided to get rid of him and find another leader. Karmakas responded by raising an army of gorgons and leading them against his own people. To punish them for their disloyalty, he wiped out all the inhabitants of his own city. As a reward for this act of cruelty, and in admiration of his treachery and wickedness, Seth, the powerful serpent-headed god he worshipped, appeared to Karmakas and gave him a cockerel's egg.

But the wizard never found time to create his basilisk. The army of the Knights of the Light, which was called in as reinforcements to rescue the humans, joined the battle against Karmakas. He hid his precious egg inside a pendant, which Yaune the Purifier then managed to steal. During the battle, Karmakas received a lance wound that pierced his body. For months he hovered between life and death, and it was many long years before he recovered his strength and powers. It was only then that Karmakas was able to start searching for Yaune and the pendant. And now his quest was finally over! Driven by his insatiable thirst for power, he would create a basilisk that would single-handedly paralyse armies and annihilate entire cities!

Karmakas spent many days locked up in his quarters, examining and caressing the pendant. Even though he now had it in his hands, he still had to bond with it psychologically and to re-energize it with his power. The time had come for the wizard to enter his chamber. He ceremoniously opened a small gold chest and took out a black phial, which had a stopper decorated with two diamond serpent fangs. Karmakas raised the little bottle towards the heavens, recited the magic formula and drank some of its contents. Almost at once, he lost consciousness and, as his head struck the floor violently, he felt his soul leave his body.

Karmakas was walking in a temple with dirty walls. He came to a chapel built entirely of human bones. The columns that supported the roof were made of skulls. Arm and leg bones, set into the walls, made it look like a morbid, terrifying tapestry. In the centre of the chapel, a serpent-headed man was sitting on a golden throne. His skin was red and his hands were like the powerful talons of an eagle. Karmakas knelt before Seth, the god of jealousy and treachery.

'Your ssslave is here, most powerful Ssseth. I bring you good newsss. Do you wish to hear it?'

The god blinked his eyes twice to indicate 'yes'.

'I have found the pendant containing the cockerel'sss egg,' the naga went on. 'In a few hoursss I will have a basilisk in my possession. With thisss at the head of my army of gorgonsss, neither the humansss nor the creaturesss of the light will be able to resist usss.'

'That is good news,' replied the god. 'The war has begun. All the gods of evil will unite at last to take over the world. At this very moment, our water-creatures are conquering many of the aquatic kingdoms. We are counting on you, Karmakas, to spread the power of darkness over the earth. You are one of our most loyal servants and we hold you in high esteem. But be careful. Remember the Lady in White has recreated the ancient tradition of the mask wearers, and a young warrior of balance has taken up the torch. Soon you will receive a visit from this chosen one. As yet he is not strong and has limited powers. You must eliminate him quickly, along with his pathetic little army!'

Karmakas stood up, bowed to his master and left the sinister chapel. Back in the castle, he woke with a start as his soul returned to his body. Weary from the journey, the naga rose and made his way to his laboratory in the cellars, where he kept his potions, phials of poison and a thick, black book. Seizing the pendant, he broke it between his powerful fingers and retrieved the cockerel's egg. Much smaller than a hen's egg, it was pale green and speckled with grey, and its shell was as hard as stone. Karmakas placed it in a wooden box with air-holes in the lid. Then, from another box he took a huge toad, which he sat on top of the egg. He closed the box.

Once he had completed his task, Karmakas went back upstairs to the great hall and commanded that Medusa be brought to him. Minutes later, she stood before him.

'You summoned me, father?' she asked.

'Yes,' said Karmakas. 'Lissssten carefully. I have another mission of the utmost importance for you. I know that an army will arrive here sssoon to reclaim the sscity. You will go and interssscept it. Among the sssoldiers will be a human with the title of masssk wearer. You must win hisss confidence and then turn him to ssstone. When he has been petrified, I will sssend hordes of sssnakes to destroy his army and then the gorgons will take care of the sssurvivors. Go now – and don't return until you have accomplished your mission!'

Medusa couldn't believe her ears. She had only just heard Amos' message in the grotto, and Karmakas already knew most of what it said. How had he found out so quickly that an army was on its way? She feared her father's great power. Every time she saw him, she trembled from head to foot, but if she wanted to live she had to obey him. It took all her courage to remain calm.

'I will try to satisfy you as best I can,' she answered.

'Leave me now. I have other thingsss to do,' he said, slithering away.

Then, absorbed in his thoughts, he added dreamily: 'My basssilisk is waiting for me!'

CHAPTER SIXTEEN

THE ARMY OF BERRION

For four days Amos drilled the Knights of Balance in preparation for their mission. Their shields were polished until, like mirrors, they reflected everything before them. By the time the blacksmiths of Berrion had finished with them, the tall, rectangular shields of the infantry and the round shields of the archers glinted in the sun.

A careful reading of *Al-Qatrum, the Territories of the Netherworld*, had given Amos a most unusual battle strategy. The Lady in White had warned him that the enemy was planning to rain a shower of poisonous vipers down on them, so Amos commanded that each knight was to be given two mongooses – the snake's greatest enemy. After combing the territory of Berrion and all the surrounding kingdoms, they managed to capture seven hundred and seventy-seven of these creatures and distribute them among the four hundred soldiers. The men were ordered not to feed their mongooses too much during the journey to Great Bratel – the snake-eaters had to be hungry when they met their enemy!

Amos also needed a cockerel, and out of all of the birds in Berrion, he chose the one with the shrillest, most powerful voice. Thanks to his power over birds, the cockerel followed him faithfully everywhere he went.

Junos trusted Amos' tactics and obeyed the boy's instructions without question. He was delighted to be leading his men, and even hired a bard, who sang and played rousing ballads to keep up morale. And so it was in a festive mood that Amos and his army set out from the city of Berrion to free Great Bratel from the gorgons.

When they saw the Knights of Balance approaching, their banners fluttering in the breeze, the inhabitants of every town and village came out to greet them with loud applause. They had all heard about the mission and wanted to cheer their brave heroes on.

As Urban and Frilla were not warriors, they could not help on the battlefield, so they remained in Berrion to await Amos' return. They had every confidence in their son and freely let him take charge of his own fate.

For five long days the soldiers of Berrion galloped from daybreak to sunset. On the evening of the fifth day they arrived at the boundary of the kingdom of the Knights of the Light. Scouts were sent ahead to Great Bratel, where a terrifying spectacle awaited them.

The road leading to the capital was lined on both sides by hundreds of stone statues, like a macabre guard of honour. It was plain to see that all of the inhabitants of the city – men, women, children and animals – had been petrified.

When the scouts returned with their grisly report, the army lost some of its confidence and spirit. The soldiers knew that somewhere ahead was a powerful enemy capable of the most devilish feats. After conferring, Amos and Junos decided it was too late in the day to go much further. They set up a makeshift camp and assigned men to stand guard for the night.

Junos tried in vain to raise his men's spirits. Most of them had had little experience on the battlefield and felt helpless against the dangers ahead. Even the bard had stopped singing and begged to be allowed to go home. When the sun disappeared below the horizon, Amos and Junos sat by the campfire discussing strategy.

'Excuse me, Master Daragon,' interrupted a guard. 'There's a rather strange girl here who wants to talk to you. Will you see her, or should I send her away?'

Intrigued, Amos said he'd meet the unexpected visitor. She was brought before him surrounded by four knights. She wore a cape with a big hood that completely hid her eyes, but Amos noticed with dismay that little golden snakes were writhing beneath it. A few paces away, the mongooses were growing restless in their cages. Amos turned abruptly to Junos.

'She's a gorgon!'

Junos immediately began shouting at the top of his voice:

'Guards! Raise the mirror-shields! We have a gorgon in the camp!'

Within seconds the girl was surrounded by mirrors. She threw herself face down on the ground, her whole body trembling.

'Please,' she begged, 'don't hurt me! My name is Medusa. I'm alone and I come as a friend! Don't hurt me, I beg you! Tell Amos Daragon I've come to help and that I know his friend Beorf! Please! I assure you I mean you no harm!'

Amos was amazed to hear the name of his friend Beorf. The newcomer seemed to be sincere, but for safety's sake he commanded that she be blindfolded and her hands tied behind her back. The guards took her into the light of the campfire where he could see her properly. About twenty knights surrounded Medusa, their shields turned towards her so that she could not escape without coming face to face with her own reflection.

Amos strode over to her.

'I am Amos Daragon. You wanted to talk to me? Go ahead, I'm listening.'

'I said I knew your friend Beorf,' answered Medusa. 'I've come to tell you that he's now a stone statue.

And I'm the one who did it! But don't judge me now, let me tell my story and you might understand.'

Stunned, Amos staggered back and fell. It was all his fault! He should never have left without Beorf! He had left his friend to face a terrible danger alone, and the poor manimal had paid dearly for it. For an instant, Amos was tempted to order the knights to kill the young gorgon, but he managed to control himself.

'Go on,' he said to Medusa, holding back his tears. 'I'm listening.'

'The magician you are preparing to do battle with is called Karmakas. Like your friend Beorf, he belongs to the species of manimals. He can transform himself into a serpent and he has power over all kinds of reptiles. He also controls the snake-hair of the gorgons, which is why they must serve him as slaves. It was Karmakas who sent me here to charm you and then turn you to stone, just like I did to your friend.

'When he was captured by Karmakas, Beorf refused to tell him where he had hidden the pendant. So I was told to free him in order to gain his confidence. Once I'd done that, I was meant to get the secret out of him. Anyway, I freed him, we took refuge in a grotto and spent days getting to know each other. Beorf soon fell in love with me. But I had to be careful because I knew that Karmakas was listening to all our conversations, waiting for the right moment to strike. When Beorf trusted me enough to reveal his secret, Karmakas came out of the shadows and forced him to fetch the pendant. Once he'd got his hands on that, Karmakas made me transform Beorf into a stone statue. It was only afterwards that I realized how much I missed him.

'I couldn't stop thinking about him. Since then, I have returned to the grotto every day to see his statue. Now I know what friendship – perhaps even love – is. This feeling does not exist among the gorgons. It's been a great revelation for me. I regret what I did and I've come here to redeem myself. I'm prepared to betray Karmakas and give you secrets that will help defeat him.'

Amos, touched by Medusa's story, was silent for a moment.

'But that won't bring my friend back,' he sighed.

'He told me a lot about you,' said the young gorgon. 'I know that you're not easily discouraged and I know a way to bring him back to life. Win this battle, reclaim the city, and I will restore your friend to you just as you knew him.'

'How can I trust you after what you have just told me?' asked Amos. 'How do I know this isn't another of Karmakas' tricks?'

'Let me finish, then you can judge for yourself how honest I've been. I know Karmakas' plans – he's going to attack you soon. Once you get close to Great Bratel, even if you stay out of sight, he will sense your presence.

He's planning to send torrents of venomous vipers raining down on you. I know these creatures – one bite sends a victim into a deep coma. The poison slowly works its way into the heart and stops the blood flowing. If you're bitten, it's certain death. I also know that Karmakas has something called a basilisk. I can't tell you what that is, though; I only heard of it a few days ago.'

'So I was right!' said Amos, frowning. 'The pendant did contain a cockerel's egg! Now I know just what kind of power he has.'

'That's good, because he won't hesitate to use it against you. And that's not all. Inside the walls of the city, there's an army of two hundred gorgons who just can't wait to fight. They're bored and squabbling with each other. They've emptied the armouries and have swords, bows, lances and clubs. You and your men seem to know how to go about killing gorgons – I realized that as soon as I heard the order to raise the mirrors! You should know that this is also the only way to bring victims back to life. Anyone who has been turned to stone is freed from the spell if the gorgon responsible is killed by seeing her own reflection. I regret that...'

'If I understand correctly,' Amos interrupted, 'the only way to free Beorf from your curse would be for you to look in a mirror?'

'I know how to free Beorf,' Medusa answered gravely. 'Trust me. Let me redeem my mistakes by helping, and I promise to return your friend to you. Consider me an ally – you really need my help. I have an idea how to trap the wizard. With my knowledge and your cunning, we can make things hard for Karmakas.'

CHAPTER SEVENTEEN

THE BATTLE

Just before sunrise the army of the Knights of Balance, led by Lord Junos, arrived at Great Bratel. The night had been short for the men of Berrion. Heavy clouds hid the stars and the pale light of early dawn glowed ominously on the horizon. The sky, like the earth, was grey. This sinister atmosphere filled the knights' hearts with dread. Even Junos had lost his usual good humour.

From atop the castle's highest turret, Karmakas watched with delight as the knights of Berrion took up their positions in the fields. The wizard caressed the head of his basilisk, then put it back in the golden cage at his feet.

'Patience, my little treasure,' he said lovingly. 'It will sssoon be time for you to act.'

Raising his arms he recited, in an ancient tongue, a magic formula several times over. The knights on the plains below watched as a black cloud formed above the city.

'Stay in your saddles and prepare to retreat,' Junos called to his men. 'If Amos is right, we'll easily win this first round!'

Karmakas continued his incantations. A powerful wind rose over Great Bratel, slowly pushing the black cloud towards the army. Suddenly, halfway between the walls of the city and the place where the men of Berrion stood, the cloud burst with a deafening clap of thunder. Hundreds of asps and cobras fell from the sky like a shower of writhing, wriggling bits of rope. The horses reared up in fear, and several knights almost retreated, but Junos galloped in front of his men, crying:

'Hold your positions! Stay where you are!'

As soon as the snakes touched the ground, they began slithering towards the army. No one moved. The snakes advanced through the tall grass like a huge ocean wave rushing towards the shore.

'Ready with the cages!' ordered Junos.

The snakes were barely a few metres from the leading horses as the knights brought out the mongoose cages. Karmakas, high on his perch, watched the scene with delight. He rubbed his hands and laughed, convinced that his snakes would finish off these arrogant humans in no time.

Then Junos shouted: 'Release the mongooses!'

The doors of all four hundred cages opened at the same time and seven hundred and seventy-seven hungry little carnivores pounced on the reptiles. They'd hardly eaten for a week. The knights galloped away at full speed and left them to it. The mongooses, more agile than the snakes, leaped into the air to avoid their fangs. With each attack they inflicted fatal wounds. Quick as lightning, they pinned the cobras to the ground with their paws while their powerful teeth crushed the snakes' heads. They caught asps by their tails and swung them in the air until they were dizzy, then held them down and finished them off. Even though the mongooses were outnumbered, the reptiles were completely overwhelmed. There was nowhere to flee, no place to hide.

The battle lasted barely ten minutes. A handful of mongooses had lost their lives, but thousands of snakes lay dead in the grass. As Karmakas watched, dumbfounded, the surviving mongooses began their feast.

The wizard was seething with rage. He stamped about, screaming insults in naga language and slapping his head in disbelief. How could they have known about the cloud of snakes? He had used this magic trick often, and there were never any survivors! Seeing the men of Berrion, unharmed, taking up their positions in the field again, he snarled through clenched teeth:

'Sssss. Now you will truly meet your end!'

Karmakas opened the basilisk's cage and took the terrible creature in his hands.

'Go and sssmash that gang of court jestersss to a pulp!'

Amos and Medusa were hidden in the tall grass, not far from the walls of Great Bratel. From this strategic front-row position the mask wearer had a perfect view of the city gates through his telescope, and could send orders to Junos in an air ball. Satisfied with what the mongooses had accomplished, he waited confidently for what was to come next. With the cockerel on his lap, he was ready for stage two. He was banking on Karmakas releasing his basilisk right away.

Suddenly, the city gates opened by just a crack. Something the size of a large chicken emerged. The basilisk was identical to the description Amos had read in his book. It had a cockerel's comb and a vulture's beak, and it walked on two skinny, featherless bird-feet like those of a chicken. But its body was that of a serpent! The basilisk spread its wings...

At that same moment, Amos and Medusa plugged their ears with a thick fern-paste. Amos sent a few words by air ball to Junos, who cried to his men:

'Plug your ears!'

Immediately, all the knights plugged their ears with fern paste. Everything was going exactly to plan: nothing had been left to chance. As the basilisk took flight, Amos saw its beak open and knew the creature was about to utter its terrible, paralyzing cry. As it did so, Medusa quickly grabbed the spyglass. With a nod, she confirmed to Amos that the soldiers were unaffected. Only the horses had been immobilized.

Concentrating hard, Amos created a message-sphere in his right hand. With the other hand, he sent a strong wind blowing against the basilisk. However hard it beat its wings to reach the knights, the wind was too strong. The basilisk was brought to a virtual standstill. Amos, concentrating hard, continued to direct the wind. He had practised a good deal in Berrion before leaving, but the feat was draining all his energy and the intense concentration gave him a bad headache.

The basilisk was still striving to move forward, but Amos was too strong for it. Great beads of sweat ran down the mask wearer's face. His faithful cockerel was standing close beside him, quite unconcerned. Amos was waiting for the right moment before he signalled for it to crow! Holding the air ball firmly in his right hand, Amos felt his legs weaken as he raised his left hand. He was slowly losing control over the wind, and the basilisk was gaining ground. To slow it down, Junos gave a signal and a flight of arrows soared towards the creature. It swerved clumsily.

Karmakas watched the spectacle with his teeth clenched. Froth began to form at the corners of his mouth. He could not understand why the wind had risen, or why the knights were still able to move! A second volley of arrows flew through the air, wounding the basilisk in the leg. But the blow only seemed to increase its strength, and it flew on strongly against the wind towards the army of Berrion.

Suddenly, the cockerel let out a resounding 'cock-a-doodle-doo'! As it crowed, Amos neatly trapped its cry in his air ball. But as he did so, he lost concentration and the wind dropped suddenly. The basilisk dived headfirst towards the knights. A glance from its dreadful eyes set the men's hair and beards alight and singed the manes and tails of the horses. Exhausted, Amos just managed to hurl his sphere at the terrible creature.

'Here,' he shouted, 'I have a message for you!'

What happened next sent tears of rage running down Karmakas' cheeks. The cockerel's crow, trapped in the air ball, hit the basilisk's head and seeped into its ears. Only the flying creature itself heard the cry – the last sound it heard before it blew into a thousand fragments in mid-flight.

Shouts of victory arose from the knights, who were already unplugging their ears and congratulating each other in a flurry of handshakes and embraces. Amos just had time to smile before he passed out, exhausted by his efforts.

When he came to, he had been carried to a makeshift shelter and Medusa was at his side. Her hood still hid her eyes but from under it she was softly humming a melody from her country.

'What happened? Where am I?' asked Amos.

'Ah, you're awake at last. You've been sleeping for two days!' answered Medusa.

Amos leaped to his feet, panic-stricken.

'Two days? I've been sleeping for two days?'

'Yes,' said the gorgon. 'But don't worry, the knights have taken care of everything.'

'Tell me! Tell me everything that's happened, right down to the last detail,' he implored.

'We have the situation under control,' Medusa began. 'Once the basilisk was dead, Karmakas sent dozens of pythons and boas down over the walls. They were huge, with bodies as thick as tree trunks. But the knights had got their confidence back after winning the first two attacks and they really went for them. It was a hard battle – several of our men were wounded – but Junos was magnificent. He was yelling orders and swinging his sword – he alone killed a good dozen! It was thanks to him that we won. Then, a few minutes later, there was what felt like a small earthquake inside the castle. No one knows what happened.'

'But what's happening now?' asked Amos anxiously.

'The knights have worked day and night. They've dug trenches and put up wooden barricades. They're on patrol constantly, and have lit fires that burn round the clock. But they're very tired – they're even falling asleep on guard duty. They keep their mirror-shields directed towards the city, though, and not a single gorgon dares to peek out. But Karmakas must be planning to launch another attack against us. We can't capture the city because the walls are too high. The gorgons shoot arrows at anything that moves. Trying to get close to the walls would mean death, and we'd never manage to break down the gates. Junos doesn't know what to do next. He could hardly wait for you to wake up and devise a new strategy.'

'Fine,' said Amos. 'Unlike the knights, I'm well rested. And I do have a plan. Tell me where Junos is and we'll finish this battle in a few hours.'

Karmakas returned to his laboratory completely baffled. For the first time in his life he had lost three consecutive battles. For a wizard as powerful as himself, this was unheard of. He fumed with shame and pounded the table with his fist. Blinded by rage, he did not notice that the room was changing. Human skulls, arm and leg bones now adorned his laboratory walls. In an instant, Karmakas knew that the god Seth had left his own world to come and speak with him. He turned slowly to see the god sitting comfortably on his golden throne, looking contemptuously at Karmakas.

'Is this how you treat me?' he said, crossing his legs.

'I give you a cockerel's egg and you, you third-rate magician, allow it to be stolen by the stupid Knights of the Light. Then, after years of searching, you finally find my precious gift again. You manage to hatch it – and then lose your basilisk! Pathetic! How can I have confidence in you any more? How can I give you my blessing?'

Karmakas bowed his head and begged for his master's forgiveness.

'I'm sssorry. I have underessstimated my adversariesss. I thought...'

But Seth interrupted his disciple in a voice that shook the earth.

'You thought? May pestilence strike you down, vermin! Win this war, or I will crush you under my heel, you foul reptile! Now, go and show yourself worthy of my divine power and trust!'

The entire castle shook and the foundations cracked. The bone walls vanished and the chapel of Seth faded into nothing. Karmakas was alone, back in his laboratory. He fell to the floor, his head in his hands, trembling with dread and fury. He lay like this for a moment, then leaped up, grabbed his book of magic and began to study his most powerful spells. He remained locked in his laboratory for a very long time.

While Amos and Junos were making plans to take the city, Medusa made her way secretly to Beorf's grotto. The stone boy was a pitiful sight. The young gorgon tenderly stroked his head and whispered in his ear:

'You'll soon be free, Beorf. I know you can hear me. Your body may be stone but your soul is still there, waiting to be set free. I've come to see you for the last time. You are the first and only friend I ever had. I'll never see you again, but I will carry you in my heart forever. Remember my eyes – you're the only person who has ever seen them! Thank you for your friendship and your kindness. Thank you for trusting me. I will show myself worthy of your trust and your love. Goodbye, my friend.'

She kissed Beorf on the cheek and sadly left the grotto for the last time. She arrived back at the camp just as the knights were getting ready to enter the city. No one had noticed her absence. It was now almost dusk, so the men of Berrion would have to move quickly. Medusa saw that they were no longer wearing their armour. Their breastplates, helmets and boots were being worn by what looked like scarecrows. The soldiers had made a whole army of figures out of branches, mud and wood, and assembled them in front of the city. From a distance, they looked exactly like real soldiers. The enemy would have had to watch them for a long time before they realised they weren't alive.

Amos led the real warriors to the tunnel through which he had once followed Beorf under the walls of Great Bratel. Medusa also knew it well. She had used it so many times to make her way to the grotto. The knights followed in tight ranks, their swords in one hand and their mirror-shields in the other. On their belts were torches, ready to light. All the shields now had leather straps, so that the knights could carry them on their backs like tortoise shells. The entire army marched through the tunnel without being seen. Once inside the city walls, they crawled along the ground to find hiding places.

'I'll head for the castle with Medusa,' Amos said to Junos. 'She can guide me to the wizard. Wait till you hear from me – I'll give you the signal to attack.'

Solemnly, Junos shook his friend's hand.

'As you wish, Sir Mask Wearer!' he replied. 'Good luck, Amos! I think Crivannia would be very happy with her choice if she could see you now, leading this battle.'

'Thank you, Junos,' Amos answered, smiling. 'See you when it's all over!'

Medusa and Amos entered the castle. Amos had a canvas sack over his head and his hands were tied behind his back. The young gorgon was pulling him behind her at the end of a rope. She pretended to be limping, using the ivory trident as a cane to support herself.

She walked straight past the guard of gorgons and presented herself to Karmakas.

'I have captured the mask wearer, master. I've come to hand him over to you in person.'

'And why didn't you turn him to ssstone as I asssked you to?' the wizard growled.

'His powers are great, father – he resisted my magic,' she answered, bowing her head.

Karmakas went over to Amos and pulled off the sack. Seeing the boy's face, he laughed contemptuously.

'Is thisss him? Is it thisss child who has been causing me ssso much trouble? Ah well – come here and sssee what's about to happen to your preciousss army!'

Medusa stood back as Karmakas pushed Amos onto the balcony.

'Now,' he cried, 'sssee my power and watch your men die!'

The wizard raised his arms and uttered a magic spell. From the surrounding fields, a thick, yellow and green cloud arose. It covered the fields and part of the forest for at least half a league.

'Anyone who inhales the air will be poisoned and die,' Karmakas said with relish. 'Your knights will not lassst long!'

'My men are indestructible, Karmakas,' Amos answered calmly. 'Look, they're all still standing!'

He began to concentrate hard and, by sheer willpower, conjured up a steady breeze. Slowly, it pushed away the thick cloud and the wizard saw all the knights still standing in the distance. They had not budged! The poison hadn't had the least effect on them.

'Who are you?' hissed the wizard, trying to remain calm. 'Who sssent you, and how have you been able to thwart my magic ssso easily?'

'I am Amos Daragon, your worst nightmare!' the boy answered with defiance.

'Very well, let's sssee what your knights can do against thisss!'

With that, Karmakas left the room, ordering Medusa to keep an eye on the prisoner. The wizard ordered his army of gorgons to gather behind the big gates. Amos, meanwhile, created an air ball and sent a message to Junos.

'I think they're getting ready to attack. It's time!'

In the shadows of the setting sun, Junos saw the gorgons gathering at the city gates. On his command, the knights began to advance silently. As best they could, among the ruined houses and rubble-filled streets, they formed a semi-circle around the creatures. They could not afford to let a single one escape. The men of Berrion were tired and tense, but they knew if they won this final battle they would at last be able to rest and then return home.

Karmakas cleared a path through the gorgons.

'Now you will exterminate thisss miserable army for me! Open the portcullisss!'

But before anyone had time to do this, Junos shouted: 'Torches!'

Four hundred torches were lit in a single moment. The gorgons screamed with terror as Karmakas ordered them to attack the intruders. The knights advanced towards the women warriors. They walked backwards with their mirror-shields tied to their backs. They guided themselves with small mirrors held in their left hands, and they raised their right hands high, so that the light from their torches lit up the scene.

Dozens of gorgons looked at their own reflection at the same time. With dreadful screams of pain, they were torn apart from the inside and crumbled into dust. The snake-headed women were surrounded by mirrors. They raised the portcullis to flee, but on the other side, fifty knights were waiting for them, forming another wall of reflective shields. This final assault killed even more. The gorgons fell dead one after another around the wizard. The knights drew their circle tighter and tighter – not a single gorgon was allowed to escape.

By now, Karmakas had transformed himself into an enormous rattlesnake and managed to slip away, slithering up the castle tower. Furiously, he kept repeating: 'I'll get you, little mask wearer, I'm going to kill you!'

From high in the tower, Amos and Medusa watched the slaughter of the gorgon army.

'Thank you, Medusa,' said Amos. 'You have saved hundreds of human lives and this city will be reborn.'

'But now I have to tell you something important, Amos,' she answered. 'There's only one way to bring our friend back to life, and you know the method as well as I do. Listen to what I have to say, and don't move.'

The young gorgon stepped away from Amos. Her hands were trembling and her legs barely held her up.

'I know what you're going to tell me, Medusa, but I'll never force you to look at your own reflection. There must be some other way to bring Beorf back to life. We'll find it together.'

'I know what I'm talking about, Amos. I also know you won't force me to do anything against my will. You would never sacrifice me to save your friend. During these past few days we've grown close. You, Beorf and I would have made an unbeatable team. I've learned that true friendship sometimes means sacrificing yourself for others. That's what Beorf taught me when he looked into my eyes. He could just as easily have killed me with one swipe of his powerful claws. But out of friendship for me he didn't do it. Even after I betrayed him he stayed true to himself and to his feelings for me. The two of you have taught me a lot about friendship. It's the best quality humans have, and now it's my turn to demonstrate my humanity. Tell Beorf that I carry him with me in death!'

With that, Medusa pulled out the little pocket mirror she had stolen from Junos. Amos leaped forward to stop her, but it was too late. She had already looked at her own reflection.

'It's true, Beorf, I do have beautiful eyes!' Medusa whispered before crumbling into dust.

Just then Karmakas appeared in the doorway and threw himself on Amos. Instinctively the boy grabbed his trident, just managing to avoid the gigantic rattlesnake's fangs. A second attack knocked Amos to the floor. He rolled to one side, broke loose from the wizard and whispered to his trident:

'If you can do extraordinary things, now's the time to show me!'

Amos threw his weapon at the serpent with all his strength. The trident barely penetrated the rattlesnake's body. Karmakas, safe inside the scales that protected him like chain-mail, jeered at the boy.

'Ssss...Do you really think you can fight me with that? I'm going to ssswallow you – whole!'

But as he hurled himself once again at Amos, the wizard suddenly began to feel giddy. The trident, still planted in his flesh, was now glowing with a pale blue light. Karmakas vomited salt water. The trident slowly sank deeper and deeper into his body. Then, as Amos watched in amazement, water began oozing out of the walls and poured down from the ceiling in torrents. Even the floor of the room seemed to be turning to liquid. Two mermaids swam up through the water and grabbed Karmakas. Amos stood still in the water unable to believe the scene before his eyes. The mermaids trussed up the huge serpent in a seaweed net, dragged him underwater and disappeared just as quickly as they had appeared. The water drained away and, in the blink of an eye, the room returned to its normal appearance. All that remained was a broken pocket mirror lying on the floor.

CHAPTER EIGHTEEN

BARTHELEMY, LORD OF GREAT BRATEL

Beorf opened his eyes. He had the distinct impression he had been sleeping for years. He sat on the floor until he got his bearings. His stomach was growling with hunger. Scrabbling around for a few nuts, he tried to remember what had happened before he was turned to stone. He could only think of the young gorgon. During his slumber he had dreamed that Medusa had been stroking his face. Her sweet voice had often soothed his dreams. Then, the image of Karmakas forced itself into his mind. Beorf also remembered his friend Amos. Why had he left him? With a whirlwind of memories swirling around in his head, Beorf left the grotto and set off through the forest, not really knowing where he was going.

Returned to their former selves, the inhabitants of Great Bratel, the Knights of the Light and all the peasants and merchants, got up from the roadside and began to walk towards the city. They were welcomed at the gates by the men of Berrion. All the gorgons had been reduced to dust, and the evil spell was now nothing but a bad memory. Everyone gathered in the centre of the ransacked city. Standing on a makeshift platform, Junos addressed the crowd.

'People of Great Bratel! I, Junos, lord of the Knights of Balance and master of the lands of Berrion, declare this city free! We have battled evil and freed you from the power of the gorgons. I now offer to help you rebuild this city, in harmony and respect for all.'

'Away with you!' shouted a voice from the crowd. 'There's only one master here, and that's me!'

Yaune the Purifier was stalking towards the platform.

'Nobody tells the Knights of the Light what to do or how to do it. Leave now and let us rebuild our city as we wish.'

A murmur ran through the crowd. Junos raised his hand and called for silence.

'You should know, citizens of Great Bratel, that it was because of your former lord that you almost lost your lives here! Yaune the Purifier knew very well that a powerful wizard was looking for him. He hid the truth from you, and his lies almost destroyed you. A true knight never lies, yet Yaune lied to you year after year. Today I am speaking frankly so that you all know my intentions. I intend to annex the territory of Great Bratel to the lands of Berrion. Together we will create a huge kingdom...'

'Silence! Leave here at once!' cried Yaune, drawing his sword. 'I will tolerate your insults no longer!'

Then Barthelemy stepped forward.

'Yaune, shouldn't we listen to what this man has to say? We owe him our lives. Without his courage, this city would still be in the hands of our enemies. Out of respect for the exploits of his men, and to express our gratitude, I am prepared to swear allegiance to him. There's no shame in serving the strongest warrior. When a lord is just and good, a knight must submit and recognize the worth of one who asks for an alliance.'

'Traitor!' roared Yaune. 'You talk like your father! And since we're all speaking our minds, I'll admit to you now that I killed him with my own sword. Your father was with me when the pendant fell into my hands. He insisted we destroy it immediately, but I refused. I wanted to keep it for myself. He challenged me to a duel and it was his blood that spilled. Now I sentence you to be burned alive, for treason against your lord. Knights of the Light, seize him at once!'

Bewildered, the knights looked at each other.

'We've burned enough innocent people!' said one of them. 'I stand behind Barthelemy. May his punishment also be mine, since I am weary of obeying Yaune the Purifier.'

A second Knight of the Light went over to Barthelemy and placed a hand on his shoulder.

'I have known this man since my earliest childhood,' he said. 'I believe he is destined to be our new lord! I'm also in favour of an alliance with our saviours, our friends from Berrion.'

The crowd applauded wildly and all the Knights of the Light moved to stand behind Barthelemy, their new master. Junos called for silence once more.

'Great Bratel has chosen a new sovereign! Barthelemy, stand beside me on this platform and accept the acclaim of your people! I can assure you of the friendship and loyalty of Berrion. To improve trade between us, we'll build a proper road to link our two kingdoms. We'll work together to ensure the prosperity and well-being of all our people.'

In a fit of rage, Yaune raised his sword to strike Barthelemy down, but he was quickly disarmed by Junos' guard.

'Leave him!' cried Barthelemy. 'For killing my father, Yaune, I banish you. The word "murderer" will be tattooed on your forehead so everyone will know what kind of man you are. I also strip you of your privileges as a knight. Never again will anyone in this kingdom be burned at the stake. We will rebuild this city on new foundations!'

All this time Amos had been searching the crowd for Beorf. As there was no sign of him, he decided to look outside the city. It was a full moon and he could see everything around him quite clearly. As he walked across the meadows, Amos was relieved to see Beorf appear at last at the edge of the forest. He ran towards him, calling his name. Overjoyed at finding one other again, the two friends threw themselves into each other's arms.

'Amos!' cried Beorf. 'I'm so happy so see you again! But I'm looking for my new friend Medusa. I'd love to introduce you to her, but she seems to have disappeared. She was with me... It was the wizard who...'

'Beorf, we have many things to tell each other,' interrupted Amos. 'Let's sit down together and I'll tell you the most wonderful story of friendship I've ever known.'

He told Beorf everything Medusa had confided in him. Then, as gently as he could, he broke the news to his friend that Medusa had sacrificed herself for him. Beorf could not hold back his tears.

'I'll never see her again, will I, Amos?'

'No, Beorf, I'm afraid not.'

There was a heavy silence between them.

'She was so kind and so beautiful,' mumbled Beorf after a moment. 'I loved her. I spent the best moments of my life with her. Her eyes. You should have seen her eyes... But I did try my best to avoid seeing them.'

He sighed and pulled himself together. 'Okay then!' he exclaimed. 'Come on, my friend. Let's go back to the city to join the others.'

On the way, Beorf recalled that the last time he had seen Amos he was leaving for Tarkasis Forest.

'Tell me, Amos, do you know now what a mask wearer is?'

'Oh, yes, I certainly do! Watch this.'

Concentrating, he held out his arm and raised it slowly. A light breeze swirled playfully around the two friends.

***

Branded with an inscription on his forehead that he could never remove, Yaune the Purifier was locked in a wooden cage and carried to the borders of the kingdom. Then the former Lord of Great Bratel began his life on the road as a beggar. His tattoo betrayed his shame to everyone, and he was chased out of all the villages he dared to enter.

One night, without realizing it, he entered the Kingdom of Omain, Lord Edonf's domain. Yaune noticed a little chapel and went in, thinking he had found a place to rest. A shiver ran down his back as he saw that the walls and beams of the building were made from human bones. Before him, on a golden throne, sat a creature with a serpent's head. Its skin was light red and its hands were like eagles' talons.

'Who are you and what do you want?' Yaune demanded boldly.

'My name is Seth. I have a proposition for you. I offer you this sword, noble knight. It tears through armour and poisons all those who touch it. A lord like you cannot live without a kingdom. Serve me and I will offer you power and riches. You will kill Lord Edonf and conquer the lands of Omain in my name.'

'And if I refuse?' asked Yaune provocatively.

'Well, if you do not accept my offer, you will return to your miserable life as a beggar and you will die poor, hungry and forgotten. Conquer the Kingdom of Omain and I will offer you revenge on Barthelemy and Junos. You will recover your former lands as well as those of Berrion. Interested?'

Yaune smiled broadly and held out his hand.

'Give me the sword, Seth. I have a great deal of work to do!'

GLOSSARY OF MYTHOLOGY

THE GODS

Lady in White: She is a character from stories and legends found in many cultures. The Lady in White helps humans to fulfil their destinies.

Seth: In Egyptian mythology, he is the god of darkness and evil. The Egyptians associated him with the desert and often represented him in the form of an imaginary creature or a man with a monster's head. He is also associated with the crocodile, the hippopotamus and the animals of the desert.

THE CREATURES OF LEGEND

Basilisk: In Europe, the Middle East and some countries of North Africa, the basilisk was considered one of the most terrifying creatures. Since all those who had the misfortune to see it perished, its true appearance is subject to controversy. In 1553, in *Cosmographia*

Universalis, the scientist Münster described the basilisk as having eight legs and no wings at all. In the great palace of Bangkok, in Thailand, you can see a statue that faithfully represents a basilisk according to the descriptions of travellers returning from the West.

Fairy: Fairies exist in many cultures, especially those of Europe. Depending on the country, they come in various sizes. Legend relates that each fairy belongs to a flower. These creatures protect nature, and time seems to have no effect on them.

Gorgon: The gorgons are creatures of Greek mythology. In the legends, they dwell in the dry, mountainous regions of Libya. In the beginning, there were three sisters: Stheno, Euryale and Medusa. Only Medusa, the most famous of the gorgons, was mortal. She had her head cut off by Perseus.

Manimal: Manimals are known in all cultures. The most famous is the werewolf. Sometimes benign and sometimes dangerous, manimals are divided into races and species. The full moon often plays an important role in their transformation from human to animal.

Nagas: The nagas are manimals which transform themselves into snakes. Those that live in the desert are called lamiae, while the nagas are associated more with watery environments. They can reach lengths of 4.6 m in their reptilian form and live around four hundred years. They are found in the Sahara, in India and in South Asia.

Merrow: In Ireland, the inhabitants of the seas are called merrows. They are easily distinguished from other aquatic creatures because of the red feathered cap they always wear. This magic hat helps them reach their dwellings in the ocean depths. The sighting of a female merrow is considered to predict a coming storm. The merrows sometimes come ashore in the form of little hornless animals.

Mermaid: The origins of these sea creatures remain obscure. They feature in the stories and legends of many ancient cultures. They are usually beautiful women with fish-tails who bewitch sailors and cause their ships to run aground on reefs.

AMOS DARAGON

BOOK TWO

THE KEY OF BRAHA

BRYAN PERRO

English Edition by
Kathy Elgin

A division of Book House

PROLOGUE

AMOS DARAGON
THE KEY OF BRAHA

A very long time ago in the fertile lands of Mahikui, there was a wondrous city called Braha. In the Mahikui language, Mahite, this meant 'Divine Marvel of the World'. The huge pyramid that stood at the centre of the city was enough to justify this title all by itself. The Mahite people were peaceful and gentle. They had lived happily alongside each other for many centuries. However, the gods were jealous of the city's beauty and they plotted to rob the mortals of their happiness. One fateful day, they combined their powers to unleash a great disaster. A terrible sandstorm buried the city and transformed all the neighbouring lands into a dry desert. Braha, the Divine Marvel of the World, was cast into another dimension. The city became a portal for the souls of all earthly creatures that had died.

From that moment on, the city was referred to as the 'City of the Dead'. A great courtroom was built, where souls went to be judged. There were two doors in the courtroom, one leading to heaven, and the other to hell. All that remained of the original city of Braha was the tip of the pyramid that pierced through the desert sand. Legend has it that the gods planted an extraordinary tree on this same site. This tree produced fruit which could turn a mortal into a god. Two guards protected a great metal door, on which was inscribed a riddle:

> *The one who dies and comes back to life,*
> *The one who sails the Styx and finds his way,*
> *The one who answers the angel and*
> * vanquishes the demon,*
> *That one will find the Key of Braha.*

Over time, the riddle grew into a legend. Then, after many centuries, the legend gradually faded from human memory.

CHAPTER ONE

THE KEY OF BRAHA

Mertellus, a ghost, was sitting at his desk, leafing through a large book of laws. During his lifetime he had been one of the greatest judges the world had ever known. When he died, the gods renewed his appointment to the bench and Mertellus presided over the grand jury of Braha, the City of the Dead. Every night for five hundred years, Mertellus and his assistant judges Korrillion and Ganhaus judged the souls of the dead who came before them.

Dead people entered the courtroom one by one. The three judges studied their cases carefully and handed down their decisions. If the dead person had committed an evil deed, the door of hell opened to reveal a great staircase leading to the bowels of the earth. If, on the other hand, his life had been one of good deeds, kindness and compassion, he was directed to the door leading to paradise.

In most cases, the decision of the three judges was unanimous and the procedure was merely a formality. Sometimes, however, the verdict was not so clear-cut. There might, for example, be accounting errors in totting up the good deeds and the bad deeds.

The smallest complication meant that the dead person was sent back to the city of Braha to remain a prisoner there until such time as a new decision was made. This process could last for decades. They suffered greatly at being refused access to either of the doors, and wandered aimlessly through the vast city. The City of the Dead was chock-a-block with ghosts awaiting judgement, and no matter how hard they worked, Mertellus and his assistants never managed to clear the backlog. Every day new arrivals entered Braha, and the problem of ghost overpopulation became increasingly serious.

Sitting at his desk in his big comfortable chair, Mertellus leafed through the large book of laws, looking for precedents for a complicated case he was judging. An ordinary man, neither very good nor very bad, had one day refused to open his door to a woman begging for shelter. Early the next morning he found the woman dead, frozen stiff on his doorstep.

The gods of good were requesting compensation for the woman. They demanded that the man be condemned to haunt his own house until he had discharged his debt towards the needy person he had neglected. The gods of evil were demanding that he be sent immediately to hell. Mertellus grumbled impatiently, searching for a solution. Piled on the floor, on tables and chairs, library shelves and even on the windowsills around him, were the files of hundreds of equally complicated cases waiting to be resolved.

Suddenly the door to Mertellus' office opened and Jerik Svenkhamr burst in without warning. This ghost was a miserable little thief who had lost his head to the guillotine. After death he hadn't been able to re-attach it to his shoulders, so he carried it around either in his hands or under his arm. He had been sentenced to go to hell for the thefts he had committed but, when he refused to go, his lawyer had proposed that he redeem himself by serving a sentence of one thousand years of service to justice instead. That was how he came to be assigned to Mertellus as his private secretary. Jerik was clumsy and nervous. He couldn't write a single thing without making a mistake and, for the past hundred and fifty-six years, he'd been driving the great judge to despair. His sudden entrance startled Mertellus.

'Jerik! You filthy little brigand, you robber of helpless old women – I've told you a hundred million times to knock before you come in!' yelled the magistrate. 'One of these days you'll scare me to death!'

Flustered by his master's anger, Jerik tried to put his head back on his shoulders and regain his composure, but it toppled over backwards, thudded to the floor and rolled away towards the stairs. The judge could hear the head's shouts as it bounced down the steps.

'I can't – ouch! – kill you. Ooh! You're – ow! – already – ouch! – dead! Ouch! Ooh! Ow!'

Jerik ran after his head but, unable to see, he tumbled down the stairs too, knocking over a dozen or so suits of armour on the staircase and making a terrific racket.

'What did I do to deserve this?' groaned Mertellus. He was addressing the gods, but the only reply was Jerik's timid voice as he reappeared, holding his head firmly in his hands.

'Master Mertellus! Your lordship. No, I should say, enlightened master of human destinies!' said Jerik, bowing and scraping in his usual grovelling way. 'Great arbitrator of the gods and – ah, I would add – ah, wise man of the law and – '

'Just tell me why you're disturbing me!' thundered the judge. 'Get to the point, you pathetic little third-rate crook!'

Trembling with terror, Jerik tried again to put his head back on his shoulders. Anticipating a repeat performance, Mertellus quickly stopped him.

'Jerik! Come here and put your head on the desk,' he ordered. 'Now sit down on the floor. Do it! Now!'

The secretary quickly obeyed.

'Now,' said the old ghost menacingly, looking the head straight in the eyes. 'Tell me what's going on or I'll bite your nose off!'

'The great doors, they're – shall we say – how can I explain? They're – ah – they're closed!' gulped Jerik.

The judge's fist thumped him hard on the skull.

'Be more specific – I need details! Which doors?'

'Yes,' stammered the secretary, 'but it's just that – mmm – Judge Korrillion and Judge Ganhaus have sent me – ah – to tell you that the doors – you know – the two doors – the ones that lead to paradise and hell – ah – well, they're closed. What I mean is – ah – that they're impossible to open. The gods have – how can I put this? – have blocked the doors. I think – ah – I think – let's not mince words – ah – I think we're facing a catastrophe!'

Mertellus grabbed his secretary's head by the hair and ran down the stairs. When he reached the courtroom, he immediately understood the gravity of the situation. Korrillion was pulling hairs out of his beard in desperation, while Ganhaus was kicking the door savagely. The two ghosts seemed completely out of their heads. Weeping, Korrillion threw his arms around Mertellus' neck.

'We're really in hot water now!' he cried. 'The gods are against us. There are too many souls in this city. I have too many cases to process – I can't handle it! I can't take it any more, Mertellus. I'm really losing it.'

'Get me an axe!' fumed Ganhaus. 'Somebody bring me an axe! I swear I'll get these doors open somehow! An axe! Now!'

Tossing his secretary's head carelessly into a corner of the room, Mertellus told his colleagues to calm down. When they had regained their composure, the three ghosts sat down around a big oak table.

'My friends,' Mertellus began, 'we are faced with a situation beyond our combined expertise. Korrillion is right. The city is swarming with ghosts, ghouls, mummies, skeletons – hordes of lost souls in great distress. If the only exits these souls can leave by are now closed, we'll soon be facing a mass uprising. We must find a solution!'

A heavy silence fell over the room. The three judges pondered. After fifteen minutes of deep thought, Ganhaus suddenly exclaimed:

'But yes, that's it! I have it! I just remembered an old story I heard a long time ago. There used to be a key that opened these doors. Wait, I'm trying to remember… The key was created specifically in case a situation like this should occur, and it was hidden somewhere in the depths of the city. Yes, it's all coming back to me now – it was when Braha was first built, thousands of years ago. Unbeknown to the gods, the first of the great judges of the City of the Dead had the key made by a famous elf locksmith. That's it!'

Korrillion was positively bouncing with joy.

'We're saved! Let's find the key and open the doors!'

'That's probably just an old legend with no basis whatsoever,' growled Mertellus. 'We have no proof the thing actually exists.'

'Then perhaps it's not the solution,' admitted Ganhaus. 'Besides, even if it were true, the legend says that the place where the key is hidden is guarded by two powerful forces that stop anyone entering. And there's another problem. I remember quite clearly that only a living person can retrieve the key and start the machinery that opens the doors.'

'Good heavens! How do you know all this?' Mertellus asked, intrigued.

'My grandmother told me the story,' Ganhaus replied. 'She was a dotty old clairvoyant who had trouble controlling her visions. She used to wake up howling like a wolf in the middle of the night. That was when I was alive, of course, many, many years ago. My people, the gypsies, loved those gruesome tales – we spent our childhood listening to granny's stories. She was a very strange woman but everyone respected her.'

'And supposing that all this is true,' said Korrillion anxiously, 'what mortal would agree to sail the Styx, the river of death, to help a city of ghosts? Nobody can come to Braha without dying first, and nobody would risk losing his life for ghosts. Everybody knows the living are afraid of us.'

A heavy silence once again filled the room. After a few minutes Jerik spoke up warily, his head still rolling about on the floor.

'Ah – I couldn't help overhearing your conversation and – well, what I mean is – I think – that, ah – I think I know someone who could help you.'

The three judges looked at each other sceptically, ignoring him. The room fell silent again.

'As I just said, I – I can help you,' Jerik insisted. 'If one of you could – ah – perhaps if one of you could put me on the chair in the corner of the room, I would be happy to – let's speak frankly – happy to share my idea with you.'

Nobody spoke. There was no reaction from the judges, who were still trying to work out their own solution while scornfully ignoring Jerik.

'Is anyone there? – Are you still there? – Hello?' Jerik asked hesitantly.

Mertellus looked at his colleagues and shrugged.

'Why not?'

After all, they had nothing to lose. Mertellus went over to the corner of the room, grabbed Jerik's head by the hair and slammed it down on the table.

'Go ahead. We're listening.'

'If you're wasting our time,' threatened Ganhaus, leaning towards the head, 'I'll throw you into the Styx myself!'

Jerik smiled timorously.

'Ah – okay,' he quavered. 'Do you remember a wizard named Karmakas from about a month ago? We sent him to hell…'

'With the number of cases we process in a month, do you seriously think we could possibly remember everyone?' asked Korrillion irritably.

'Let me finish!' begged Jerik. 'This wizard is a bit crazy. I think – what I mean is – he wouldn't stop cursing a certain Amos Daragon. He kept saying – always, over and over – he was endlessly repeating: "I'll have your hide, you miserable mask wearer. I'll get you, Amos Daragon, and I'll boil your brains for stew!"'

'So?' asked Mertellus, exasperated.

'Ah, well,' Jerik went on, 'out of curiosity – ah, well – I did a little research in the library – the section where – how can I put this?'

'Where you aren't authorized to go!' snorted Ganhaus crossly. 'You must be talking about the library that is forbidden to subordinates. I repeat, expressly forbidden to people like you!'

Jerik was sweating profusely; large drips ran down his forehead.

'Yes – ah – yes, yes, that very one. I went in there by accident but – well – that's another story – ah – if you wish, we can discuss that later. Anyway, to get back to my search. I discovered that – what I mean is – the mask wearers are beings who are chosen by the Lady in White to re-establish – you know – re-establish balance in the world. When the gods are at war – as is currently the case – we all know – there's no secret about that – they're the ones who... what I mean is, it is the mask wearers, of course – who take charge and keep an eye on things. Their task is to re-establish balance between – ah – between good and evil – and – I think – help victims of the war of the gods. What we are experiencing here – if I can be so bold – is obviously – ah – a powerful imbalance! You will no doubt agree – with – ah – with me? We should perhaps try to – to – what I mean is – find this Amos Daragon and ask him for his help. The legend of the key is – in my opinion – the only possible solution that we have – at least – at the moment. We should try it, and entrust this – ah – this great man with solving our problem! What do you think?'

'I think we have our plan,' declared Mertellus, impressed by what he had just heard. 'However, there's one more point we must clarify. Who is to be responsible for tracking down Daragon and bringing him back here?'

They pondered for a few moments. Then all three judges turned in unison and looked at Jerik's head. Jerik realised he had just been entrusted with the mission. It was too late to protest.

'I approve this choice,' said Ganhaus, pointing to the secretary.

'I wholeheartedly support this proposal,' added Korrillion.

'Your wisdom is great, dear friends,' Mertellus smiled. 'I endorse your decision, and it is with great sorrow that I bid farewell to such a good secretary. This is the moment of truth for you, my dear Jerik! If you succeed in your mission I will release you from your sentence of a thousand years in the service of justice. I'll send you directly to paradise as you desire. If, on the other hand, you fail, then you will rot in a dungeon until the end of time!'

The three judges stood up, smirking. They had found a solution to their problem and the perfect idiot to do the dirty work. On his way out, followed by Korrillion, Mertellus turned to his secretary.

'You leave tonight.' he instructed. 'I will notify Charon, captain of the Styx boat, and Baron Samedi, who will issue you with a special travel permit for this – this Amos whatever-his-name-is, so that he can get here easily.'

Ganhaus was the last to leave the room.

'Perfect! You played your role to perfection,' he whispered to Jerik. 'They fell right into the trap. We certainly pulled the wool over their eyes! Once Seth frees my murderous brother Uriel from hell, we'll eliminate that damned mask wearer Amos Daragon, and I will keep the Key of Braha for myself. If you fail in this mission, Jerik, I swear I will make you pay dearly!'

He left, slamming the door.

'Well, I certainly put my foot in it this time!' sighed Jerik, his head still sitting in the middle of the table. 'Why is it always me who – shall we say – gets stuck with the dirty work? There really is no justice in this world!'

A division of Book House

VISIT THE AMOS DARAGON WEBSITE:

www.amosdaragon.co.uk

OR VISIT BOOK HOUSE AT:

www.book-house.co.uk

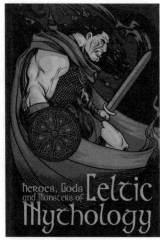

ISBN: 978-1-905638-97-0

ISBN: 978-1-906370-92-3

ISBN: 978-1-905638-29-1

ISBN: 978-1-906714-82-6

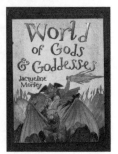

ISBN: 978-1-906714-83-3

Available at all good bookshops